Dear Reader,

Welcome to Missouri!

Certain events in life can stop us in our tracks and force us to reevaluate our lives and where we're headed. I thought I was going to my summer home in mid-Missouri for a break in my routine. However, fate has a way of jumping in and changing all our plans.

I want to share with you what happened to me one summer when I almost lost my life, my eyesight and most definitely lost my heart. I think you'll agree I made the very best of the choices given to me.

Best regards,

Damon Trent

Missouri

ANNETTE BROADRICK
Choices

Missouri

Silhouette® Books

Published by Silhouette Books New York

America's Publisher of Contemporary Romance

To Derralee Johnson,
also known in the family as "Baby Sister"

SILHOUETTE BOOKS
300 East 42nd St., New York, N.Y. 10017

CHOICES

Copyright © 1986 by Annette Broadrick

ISBN: 0-373-45175-X

Published Silhouette Books 1986, 1993, 1994

All the characters in this book have no existence outside the imagination of the author and have no relation whatsoever to anyone bearing the same name or names. They are not even distantly inspired by any individual known or unknown to the author, and all incidents are pure invention.

® and ™ are trademarks used under license. Trademarks recorded with ® are registered in the United States Patent and Trademark Office, the Canadian Trade Marks Office and in other countries.

Printed in the U.S.A.

One

Elise Brandon pushed open the swinging doors of the Intensive Care Unit of one of St. Louis's largest hospitals. She had been a staff nurse in ICU for two of her six years as a registered nurse. Elise enjoyed her profession. At thirty-two she felt fortunate to have found an occupation that fulfilled her needs and gave her a sense of contribution.

Absently touching her hand to her light brown hair tucked into a sedate chignon, Elise walked toward the nurses' station.

Diana Fuller, one of the nurses on the morning shift, looked up from the notations she was making on a patient's chart, saw Elise and smiled. "You're early."

"I know. I had trouble getting to sleep last night. The storm kept me awake. Then when I finally got to sleep I dreamed—crazy, nonsensical things." She shrugged slightly, her warm smile lighting up her face. "So I was up early, got everything done around the apartment I could think of to do and decided to come on in to work." Her glance took in several of the rooms that opened almost directly into the nursing area. The unit was set up so that the nurses' station was only steps away from any patient admitted. "It looks as though we've had several additions since I went off duty last night."

Diana brushed her dark hair away from her face. "Yes. The storm caused several accidents." She picked up one of the charts. "We've got one patient just out of surgery. He's not in very good shape." She glanced at Elise who had pulled out a chair and was sitting down beside her. "Have you ever heard of Damon Trent?"

The name sounded familiar but Elise couldn't place it. She shook her head.

"He's been written up in all the business magazines and papers: the *Wall Street Journal*, *World News*, *Time*. I just read a long article on him in *Newsweek* yesterday, then came in this morning and found him to be one of our patients."

"Is he from around here?"

"No. According to his admittance slip, he lives in Chicago. I understand he was unconscious when he was brought in last night."

"What are his injuries?"

"Concussion, ruptured spleen, collapsed lung, lacerations around the head and face, bruising in the rib and chest area."

"I take it he was in a car?"

"Yes. It was a multicar pile up on I-270. Three cars involved, two fatalities. Mr. Trent was alone. There was something in the paper this morning about it."

"I just glanced at the headlines."

"You certainly wouldn't recognize him from his pictures. I doubt that his own mother would recognize him at the moment." She looked down at the chart. "He's on a respirator, and they have tubes into his chest and ab-

dominal area.'' She motioned to the chart.
''You'll see it all here.''

''Has any of his family shown up?''

''No. A business associate, Justin Drake,
arrived before Mr. Trent was out of surgery.
He's in the waiting room at the moment.''

Diana quickly reviewed the chart of the
other patient whom Elise would be responsible for during the next shift. Fortunately the
second patient wasn't in quite so critical condition.

When she was finished Diana grinned. ''I've
got the next two days off, so I'll be seeing you
on Wednesday.'' She reached for her purse and
waved goodbye, then disappeared behind the
swinging doors.

The first thing Elise did was to check on her
patients. Mrs. Coleman was resting comfortably and Elise was fairly certain she would be
moved out of ICU within the next day or two.

Damon Trent was another matter. His
monitor was registering a rapid heartbeat, the
slight beeping noise accompanied by the hiss of
the respirator. He was as white as the linens on
which he lay, except for the rumpled black hair
that fell across his forehead. Elise could see the
faint discoloration that marked new bruises

around his face. The stark stitching that ran just above the brow line was mute evidence of how close he'd come to losing his eyes.

According to the information on his chart, he would be forty later in the year. She wondered if he'd make it to see that day. She leaned over and spoke softly.

"Mr. Trent?"

There was no response.

"Mr. Trent, I'm your nurse, Elise Brandon. You've been in an accident and are now recovering in the hospital."

She watched for sign of reaction. His eyelashes were thick and long, forming smudged crescents along his cheekbones. His face and neck were swollen.

After checking his vital signs, she returned to the nurses' desk.

A tall well-built man stood there watching her as she approached. He appeared to be in his late twenties. "Are you Damon's evening nurse?" he asked in a polite voice.

"Yes, I am."

"Has he regained consciousness?"

"According to his chart, he's out from the anesthetic, if that's what you mean."

"I was wondering if he'd know me the next time I go in?"

She smiled. "That would probably depend on whether he knew you before he had his accident, don't you think?"

"I'm sorry. I didn't introduce myself. I'm Justin Drake, Damon's second in command. But at the moment I'm not at all certain what that's going to entail. I understand his injuries are serious."

"Yes, they are."

"When may I go in to see him again?"

She checked her watch. "You may go in now if you wish. But please don't stay more than ten minutes."

He nodded. "That's what the morning nurse told me. Thank you."

She watched the tall man enter Damon Trent's room. He was very striking with his blond hair and navy-blue eyes, the kind of man who made most women look twice, and wonder if he were married. Most women, that is. But not her.

Elise glanced down at her ring finger. The imprint was finally gone and the late-spring sun had evened out the coloring so that there was no sign that she'd worn a wedding band.

She wished she could as easily remove the emotional scars caused by the memory of her marriage and its unpleasant ending.

Elise picked up Damon Trent's chart and made a few notations regarding his condition.

The next time she walked into his room, Damon was moving slightly, his hands twitching, and she walked over and placed her hand on his.

"Mr. Trent?"

His eyelashes fluttered but they didn't open.

"Mr. Trent, this is Sunday, May 9. You are in a St. Louis hospital. You were in an automobile accident last night and had surgery." Her voice was low and soothing. She stroked his hand softly. "You're going to be fine, Mr. Trent. Just fine." She found herself hoping so. What a waste to have something happen to the man at this point in his life.

While she talked to him he lay still, but when she was silent for a moment his head turned restlessly on the pillow and his hands began to pluck at the tubing.

"Mr. Trent, please don't touch the tubing."

He didn't seem to hear her and his fingers twitched spasmodically.

Elise was afraid he'd accidentally injure himself before he was fully aware of what he was doing. She leaned over closer to him. "Mr. Trent. I'm going to fasten your wrists down so that you don't harm yourself. This is for your own protection. You'll be all right, Mr. Trent."

Damon felt as though he were in a black hole filled with rhythmic noises. He heard a slight beeping sound, repeating itself monotonously over and over. It was accompanied by a steady hiss.

Where was he? His head felt as though it were being held in a vise, the slightest movement producing excruciating pain. He tried to move his arms and couldn't. They felt weighted down.

He shifted restlessly. His feet felt bound and when he attempted to move, a searing pain shot across his abdomen.

Something was wrong—drastically wrong. What had happened to him?

From a far-off distance he faintly heard a soothing voice. "You're going to be all right, Mr. Trent. You are in a hospital in St. Louis, but you're doing very well. Please lie still. You've been in an accident and you're going to be fine."

He had to concentrate to hear the voice, it was so far away. Was that what angels sounded like? Would an angel be anywhere around him if he were dead? The pain seemed to come straight from hell.

The black hole engulfed him once more.

"Ms. Brandon?"

Elise paused just outside of Damon Trent's room and looked at Justin Drake. "Yes?"

"Is he any better?"

She smiled. "He's in stable condition, if that's what you mean. He isn't getting any worse."

The man was obviously worried. He hadn't left the hospital since she'd come on duty. Visiting hours had been over an hour before and still he stayed. "Do you have a place to stay, Mr. Drake?"

"Oh, uh, yes. I checked into a motel down the street when I first got here."

"Why don't you go get some rest? I'm sure you're going to see an improvement by morning. There's really nothing you can do for him tonight."

He stared at her for a moment, no doubt assimilating what she had said. Finally, he nodded. "You're probably right." He glanced around the hallway. "If there's any change at all, could you call me?"

"Certainly." She walked over to the nurses' station and flipped open Damon's chart. "What's your number?"

"I'm staying in room 1412 at the Ramada Inn. I don't know the number."

Elise made a notation. "We'll contact you if there's any change," she reassured him. Then she watched him leave the area.

What sort of man was Damon Trent to inspire such concern and loyalty from an employee? And where were his relatives? Did he have any? She wondered if any were listed on his chart. Tomorrow she might look up the *Newsweek* article in order to learn more about him.

Elise was unaware of how unusual her interest was. She had been mechanically going through the routine of her life during the six months since her divorce was final. Had she only recognized it, she would realize her interest in her new patient was the most emotionally healthy sign she'd shown for some time.

The next afternoon Damon drifted in and out of consciousness, still suffering from his concussion. He couldn't talk with the respirator in his mouth and his eyelashes fluttered open for only seconds, then drooped once again against his pale cheeks.

However, the swelling seemed to be disappearing from around his face, giving evidence of the strong jawline that had hitherto been concealed.

Elise had read the article about him. Although there had been nothing said about his personal life, his professional career had been riveting. He'd started in construction, and after having built several malls and office buildings, he'd used the profits to take over other businesses. He seemed to have his fingers in several diversified pies.

No wonder Justin Drake was so worried. Damon Trent would be a tough act to follow.

Once again, Justin Drake had been there when Elise reported for duty that afternoon. She had nodded and smiled, but otherwise they hadn't spoken. The staff on the morning shift had allowed him to stay more than the prescribed ten minutes, hoping that Damon might recognize his voice and feel better oriented. But so far, Damon hadn't responded to verbal stimuli.

Several of the patients had been moved and the ICU was quiet. Elise found herself spending more time with the mysterious Mr. Trent. No one seemed to know why he'd been traveling in St. Louis, and no one had come forward and claimed him as kin. She refused to question Justin Drake, but recognized her curiosity for what it was—an interest in the man, not the patient.

Damon heard the voice again. It had become familiar to him, accompanying the moments when he was aware of pain and discomfort. But the voice wasn't causing the pain. *It* seemed to soothe in some way, as though the mere tone brushed softly against him in loving strokes.

A hand brushed lightly across his forehead, gently pushing the hair away from his face. When it withdrew he tried to turn his head, tried to speak, but it took too much effort. He felt so tired.

But that was why he'd planned a vacation. He'd been pushing too hard for too long and it was time to take a break. His summer place on the Lake of the Ozarks had beckoned to him.

Was that where he was? He struggled to open his eyes, but the necessary concentration created more pain. It was everywhere, in every sound, in every movement, like a weight pressing against his head, chest and body.

Elise watched Damon closely. He seemed to be stirring. She absently wondered what color his eyes were and found herself willing him to open them. Of course he couldn't speak, not with the respirator, but could he hear her?

"Mr. Trent? If you can hear me, please squeeze my hand."

She placed his hand in hers and after a moment his left thumb moved slightly. She smiled. It could have been her imagination, but she wanted so much for him to be responding. Slowly, almost imperceptibly she felt his fingers move against hers.

"There's someone here to see you, Mr. Trent. Justin Drake is here."

Justin moved closer to the bed. "Hello, Damon."

There was no response.

Justin glanced at Elise. She still held Damon's hand. "I believe he hears you. He just doesn't have the strength to respond. But it will come." Her voice sounded very confident and Justin smiled with relief.

Damon listened to the quiet, confident voice. It was low and husky, like no other he'd ever heard. It gave him a feeling of peace. Whatever was causing his pain, that voice knew he was going to be all right. He was going to be all right.

When Elise came back from her dinner break she heard voices raised in the waiting room.

"Why didn't you tell me that Damon had been hurt, Justin? Why did I have to read about it in the paper?"

"I'm sorry, Cynthia. I didn't think—"

"Don't try to excuse yourself. As Damon's fiancée I should have been the first one notified. How did you find out about it?"

"Damon carries my name and address in his wallet to call in case of an emergency. I do the same thing."

Elise glanced into the room and saw a tiny black-haired woman staring up at Justin. Her beauty was marred somewhat by the anger in her face. She was well dressed, and her tiny build made Elise, at five foot eight inches, feel like an Amazon in comparison. Elise continued back to the desk so that one of the other nurses could go eat.

A few minutes later the young woman from the waiting room appeared at the desk. "I'm Cynthia Rydell and I'm here to see Damon Trent."

Elise's jade-green eyes met the dark brown gaze of the woman across from her. In her experience Elise had always thought of brown eyes as being warm, but not in this case.

"Have you just arrived?"

"Yes."

"You may stay ten minutes, Ms. Rydell. As I'm sure you're aware, Mr. Trent is in critical condition."

The woman nodded and looked around. "Which room is he in?"

Elise stood up and motioned for Cynthia to follow her. She walked over to the bed and checked the IVs that were flowing into each of his arms. She would need to replace the one in his right arm in another ten minutes or so.

Cynthia paused in the door and stared at the man on the bed. *"That's Damon?"* she asked in a shocked voice.

"Yes."

"Oh, my God! I had no idea he'd look so awful!"

"Please keep your voice down." She glanced back at the monitor. "He may not be able to respond to you, but I'm fairly certain he can hear you."

Cynthia tiptoed over to the side of the bed and stared at Damon with revulsion. "He's going to be horribly scarred!" she said, then burst into tears.

Elise fought her natural inclination to tell the woman to get out of the room. At the moment she was treating the patient as though he were an inanimate object being viewed under a microscope. She hoped he wasn't able to follow what was being said.

Justin Drake appeared in the doorway. "Cynthia."

The woman glanced over her shoulder.

"Why don't you let me take you out for dinner? You're upset and you need a little while to adjust. We can come back later."

Cynthia stared back at Damon and shuddered. "Oh, yes. Take me out of here, please."

Elise met Justin's gaze for a moment, willing her face to stay composed. The tiny woman flung herself into his arms and he walked down the hallway with his arm around her.

"Don't pay any attention to her, Damon," she muttered while she checked the respirator and the drain. "It was just the shock of seeing you again. By the time you're out of here you shouldn't have anything to show for the accident except a few scars, and those can be taken care of by a competent plastic surgeon." She was glad none of the other nurses could hear her sounding like a mother hen to a man several years older and considerably more worldly than she.

One of the first rules of nursing was not to become emotionally involved with the patient. Elise had never had a problem with that before, but there was something about Damon Trent that tugged at her.

It was almost midnight by the time she reached her apartment. She was tired, but too keyed up to sleep. The magazine with Damon's picture lay open on her coffee table and she sat down in front of it. The photographer had taken a candid picture and had caught Damon smiling at something he was being told by the man with him. They were walking toward the camera, Damon in a light-colored suit, his dark hair burnished by the sun. His smile was very attractive—warm, free and full of enjoyment. Elise wondered what it would be like to have him smile like that at her.

She still couldn't see the color of his eyes and she tried to imagine them. Would they be black like his hair? Or perhaps blue?

A picture of Cynthia Rydell became superimposed in her mind over the picture. His fiancée. Obviously she hadn't been at her best this evening. It had been a shock to see him, particularly while he was still hooked up to all of the machines.

Elise wondered how she would have felt if that had been Guy Brandon lying there in the bed. Guy Brandon, her husband for eight years, the man she had loved with all her heart; the man she had vowed to live with for the rest of her life, to honor and cherish; the man who had made the same promises to her. She had believed him because she had believed *in* him, had always looked for the best in him and accepted his explanations without question.

What if that had been Guy?

In some ways, she felt as though Guy *had* died because the man she thought she had married really didn't exist. How many times had he told her how disgusted he became in his business watching other men lie to their wives and play their cheating games? He had repeatedly told her how thankful he was they didn't have that type of marriage, even though he did travel for a living.

Guy Brandon owned a travel agency in St. Louis and there were times when he accompanied the guides to make certain the tours were being run smoothly. Elise always had counted the days until he returned. They celebrated his homecoming like newlyweds, with Guy assuring her he saw nothing on his travels that could begin to compare with what he had waiting for him at home. And she had believed him.

Elise learned a great deal from that relationship—about herself, her expectations, and about the man she had thought would always be her other half. Elise discovered the painful part of loving and decided it wasn't worth having a relationship that close, that intense. The honesty and faithfulness had only come from her. Guy had accepted them, no doubt appreciated them and counted on her trust in him and her lack of suspicion in order to lead a carefree bachelor existence when he was traveling.

But no more. Her marriage was over and done with. Elise could only assume that Guy had found someone else to practice his charm and wit on. She had almost gotten through all the pain of betrayal and heartache. She had managed to pick up the pieces and get on with her life. But this time she intended to do it alone.

Her thoughts returned to Damon Trent. She recognized that one of the reasons she was allowing herself to feel something for him was because he was only in her life temporarily. She could use her energies in helping him to overcome the trauma he had experienced without feeling committed to him, or expecting anything in return.

From now on, Elise Brandon intended to play it safe. No more involvements—and no more pain.

Two

"Mr. Trent has decided to make his presence known," the day nurse announced as Elise came on duty the next day.

Elise glanced into his room. "He's awake, then?"

"After a fashion. We aren't getting much response from him, but what can you expect? He can't talk, but he's certainly being difficult. We had to restrain him again. He kept trying to pull the respirator out."

Elise went over the reports with the nurse going off duty and noted that Damon's vital signs had improved. If he was trying to remove the respirator, he probably didn't need it. She recognized her sense of relief that he was better with a slight sense of surprise. Making a note to check with the doctor regarding the respirator, she began her day at work.

When she walked into his room Damon turned his head toward the door. For the first time she saw his eyes. They were gray—a clear, crystal color that picked up the afternoon sunlight slanting through the window. She smiled at him but he continued to stare at her with no expression, his eyes like opaque pools.

"Good afternoon, Mr. Trent. I'm glad to see you're awake today."

There was that voice again. It had a special lilting quality that caught at him. Why wouldn't they turn on a light in here? He couldn't see a blasted thing!

She took his hand. "I know it must be frustrating for you not to be able to talk. If I get you a pencil and paper, would that help?"

A pencil and paper. How about some damned light? He felt like hell, his head ached and his stomach felt as if he'd been gored by a bull, and now he was expected to write something!

He nodded his head. Elise smiled at the frown on his face. He looked quite ferocious but he was obviously feeling better. Within minutes she was back and extended the paper to him. He didn't look at it.

"Mr. Trent?"

His head turned toward her voice.

"Here's the paper and pencil. Tell me how I can help you?"

He continued to stare at her, his eyes looking through her, and a sudden frisson of fear shot through her. She deliberately waved her hand in front of his face. He didn't flinch.

He was blind.

Calling on all of her professional skills and training, Elise forced herself to become objective. She put the pencil in one of his hands, the paper in the other. "Mr. Trent, please write down your answers to some questions for me, will you do that?"

He nodded slightly. Her voice sounded so caring, so full of warmth that he almost felt as though he could hold his hands up to her and feel the warmth. He had something in his hands, what was it? The paper was on some sort of clipboard. He couldn't see it, couldn't she understand that?

Wait a minute. Maybe it wasn't the light in this room. Was it his eyes? Good God! Was there something the matter with his eyes? He grasped the pencil and felt for the paper. In a wobbling, slanting line, he wrote, "Is there something wrong with my eyes?"

"I don't really know, Mr. Trent. I'll call the doctor and have him check. You received a strong blow to your forehead, there are stitches there." She patted his hand. "I'll be right back."

She had the doctor paged and explained what she had discovered. He said he would be there within fifteen minutes and in the meantime, to try to keep the patient calm.

Easier said than done. Didn't Damon Trent have enough problems without losing his sight as well?

Elise returned to the room, pausing in the doorway. Damon lay staring straight before him while his hands made circular motions before his face. "The doctor will be here shortly," she offered. Walking over to the bedside, she asked, "How does your head feel?" She watched him fumble for the pencil lying beside him on the bed. Then he picked up the paper and wrote, "Like hell."

She chuckled. "I'm sure it does."

He heard the light tinkle of her laugh. It made him want to smile as well. Her voice had such a soothing quality to it, as though nothing very bad could happen because she wouldn't allow it.

"What's wrong with my eyes?" he scrawled almost on top of the other writing.

"That's what the doctor is going to check, in just a few moments. You're really doing quite well, Mr. Trent, considering this is only your second day out of surgery."

"Why was I in surgery?" he wrote.

"You had a ruptured spleen." She paused, uncertain of how much to remind him. "Do you remember your accident?"

Accident? He was in a hospital, hadn't someone told him that? And he'd had surgery for a ruptured spleen? What could he remember about an accident?

He lay there, trying to think back to a time when he wasn't lying in the dark and in pain. He seemed to have been there forever.

"What is your name?" she asked softly.

Without hesitating he wrote, "Damon Trent."

At least his cognitive powers were operating. "You were in an automobile accident Saturday night. Today is Tuesday, May 11. Do you remember being in the accident?"

That's right. He'd been in the Porsche. He'd left Chicago about six o'clock, determined to get to the lake that night. He'd crossed the Mississippi around ten o'clock, during a hellacious thunderstorm that had carried high winds and smatterings of small hailstones. But that was all he could remember.

Reluctantly he wrote, "I don't remember the accident."

"That's not unusual," she reassured him. "I just wondered. You were knocked unconscious."

Then she remembered his visitors. "Mr. Drake and your fiancée are here, waiting to see you. Would you like for them to come in?"

"My fiancée?" he wrote.

"Yes."

He shook his head wearily, obviously tiring. With some effort he wrote, "I don't have a fiancée."

For just a moment Elise experienced elation that the selfish young woman wasn't going to be this man's wife, but then she realized that he could still be somewhat confused.

"She said her name is Cynthia Rydell."

Damon lay there with his eyes closed. She had just about decided he had dozed off when he wrote, "Cynthia is not my fiancée, never was, never will be."

Elise grinned at the terse message and took the paper and pencil from him. It might be more diplomatic to remove his unloverlike message before he had visitors.

"The doctor will be here momentarily. After he's checked you I will send Mr. Drake and Ms. Rydell in." She started to move away from the bed and his hand caught at hers. She paused. He shook his head. Puzzled, she handed him the paper. He felt for the pen in her other hand and wrote, "I don't want Cynthia in here."

Well, there was certainly nothing ambiguous about that statement, but Elise was a little concerned about carrying out the instructions. She had a pretty good idea that Cynthia would not take well to being told she couldn't see him.

She removed the paper once again. "All right." She absently patted his hand and left the room.

Damon lay there quietly, thinking about the woman who'd just left. He didn't even know her name, or what she looked like, but he felt that he knew her. It was her voice that had first spoken to him in the black abyss of his dark new world. It had been her touch on his forehead that had soothed him. And it was the light floral scent of her cologne that announced her presence in his room, even when she didn't speak.

Who was she? He would have to ask Justin. Then he remembered, he couldn't say anything. He couldn't see anything. Never had Damon Trent felt so helpless in all of his life!

As it turned out, Damon Trent didn't have any company during the rest of Elise's shift. Instead, he was taken upstairs for testing. By the time he was returned to his room, he was asleep. The doctor sat down at the desk and began to write in his report. The blow to the head had obviously created a blockage from the optic nerve. Surgery could be performed, but not until Damon Trent had recovered from his other injuries.

For the time being, he would have to accept the fact that he couldn't see.

Elise went off duty that night very subdued. Her conversations with Justin Drake and Cynthia Rydell hadn't helped matters.

She had to explain to them that he was having tests made and wouldn't be allowed visitors for several hours. Cynthia did not take the message well.

"I've been waiting to see him for the past two hours and now you tell me I can't even see him at all today?"

"That's correct."

"Well, let me tell you something, Nurse, your supervisor is going to hear about this. I've never seen such incompetency in all my life."

Justin Drake stepped forward. "What sort of tests are they running?" His voice reflected his concern.

"There seems to be some question as to his vision," Elise admitted.

Cynthia interrupted. "Don't tell me he's blind, for God's sake. What have you people been doing to him!"

Justin ignored the outburst. "How soon will they know something?"

Elise answered. "I'm not sure. Perhaps not before tomorrow. We have no idea how extensive the damage is at the moment."

Justin turned to Cynthia. "Let me take you back to your hotel. We can come back in the morning. Perhaps even talk to the doctor."

Elise wondered how she was going to follow Damon's instructions of keeping Cynthia out of his room. She could leave a notation in his chart that he didn't want her visiting him. After that, it was up to the nurse on duty.

Perhaps it was just as well that Elise had the next two days off. She recognized that she was getting too involved with the patient, which wasn't good for either of them.

By the time she crawled into bed that night, she was determined to forget everything—her work, her concern for Damon Trent and her lack of plans for the rest of her life.

The ringing phone brought her out of a deep sleep the next morning. She fumbled for the phone and looked at the clock sitting beside it. It was after ten o'clock, but then she hadn't gone to bed until almost two. "H'lo."

"Hi, babe, how have you been?"

Just what she needed to start off her day, a cheery call from her former husband.

"Hello, Guy."

"Say, did I wake you up?"

"Yes."

"I'm really sorry. I've tried calling several times in the evening, but never got an answer."

"I'm working the evening shift now."

"Oh, I thought maybe you had a boyfriend keeping you tied up in the evenings." He laughed at the suggestion.

He knew better. During the eight years of their marriage she had never looked at another man, never even thought about another man, and because Guy had professed to sharing the same feelings, she had thought he felt the same way toward her. When the shock had finally worn off and she had forced herself to face that he'd been living a double life—the faithful husband at home and the freewheeling lover on the road—Elise knew it would take her a long time to recover her respect for him or any other male.

Not that she hadn't had immediate offers from "friends," all willing to console her. How ironic that the married men of her acquaintance would think she would encourage

them—after having lived with a man who be-
haved in the same way!

"Why are you calling, Guy?"

"Because I've missed you and wanted to see
how you're getting along."

And no doubt hoped she wasn't able to
manage without him. For a few weeks after her
life had exploded in front of her like a land
mine, Elise had wondered how she could ever
manage without him. She had loved him so
much. She had centered her life around him
and his travels, waiting patiently for him to
return to her.

They had had a warm, loving relationship
and he had taunted her with that when she had
asked him to leave. He had reminded her that
he was the only man who had ever made love
to her and that she would never forget him,
would always want him. His taunts had given
her the backbone needed to decide to move out
and find an apartment. She was forced to face
the fact that she hadn't known the man with
whom she had spent the past several years. He
was nothing like the man he had pretended to
be. Guy Brandon was all charm and good
looks, with nothing to back him up—no character, no conscience and no integrity.

For a while Elise had hated herself for being so gullible for so long, for ignoring the signs and accepting his word.

Now she felt nothing, nothing at all, except disgust that he had managed to wake her up on a day when she could have slept in.

"I'm fine, Guy, just fine."

There was a long pause, then he finally asked in a soft voice, "Don't you even want to know how I've been?"

"Not particularly."

He ignored her comment. "Well, I'll tell you, babe. I made a big mistake, losing you. A big one. I can't tell you how much I've missed you. Waking up each morning and finding you gone has really been tough on me."

"I'm sure that waking up with Merrilee has had its compensations."

"With who?"

"Please, Guy, don't continue the pretense. I know you and Merrilee were an item for over a year before I finally caught on. And I know that you moved her into our house within a week after I moved out."

"Elise! You don't honestly believe that, do you? Someone's filling your head with a bunch of lies about me."

"Are they, Guy? Isn't it interesting how so many people who know you seem to have so many lies to tell about you?"

"They're just jealous of what you and I had together. We were an unbeatable team, you know that. We share something that no one else has ever found."

Elise laughed. The man was unbelievable. "Yes. I shared you with every tour guide and office assistant who caught your eye. I know that now. But it's certainly not anything I intend to treasure."

"You're never going to trust me again, are you?"

"Guy, how many times have we had this conversation in the past nine months?"

"What do you mean?"

"I mean that, periodically, you make these calls, say the same things and end up asking me to come back to you. When are you ever going to discover that I don't want you back? I will never want you back. I was the only one committed to our relationship and now that it's gone, I have no desire to ever work at it again."

"Can you honestly say you don't still love me? Because I love you, babe. I always will."

"Whatever that means to you. I neither know nor care at this point. No, Guy, I don't love you."

The line was silent for quite a while. Finally, she heard him sigh. "Can we at least be friends?"

"Friends? For some reason I don't really think so. I can't really picture you as a friend I could turn to in times of trouble or need. Guy, I have no friends who would ever have subjected me to the multitude of lies and deceit that you have. I don't believe I've ever had any *enemies* that relentless."

"You know, Elise, I really didn't call to listen to this kind of talk. I needed a friend and I thought you were one."

"I guess you found out differently."

"Yes. I won't bother you anymore."

"I'd appreciate that."

She heard the click of the receiver and wearily dropped hers back in the stand.

It had been almost three months since his last call. Perhaps he would get the message this time. He completely ignored the fact that they were divorced, as though it meant nothing. It probably didn't to him. The marriage had meant nothing to him, either.

Elise rolled over in the bed and forced herself to relax. Today was her day off. She might sleep for a while longer, then do some shopping, meet a friend for a drink later in the day, take in a movie that night. After eight years of thinking like one half of a couple, she was finally beginning to enjoy thinking single.

And the one thing she knew with certainty was that she had no intention of getting emotionally involved with anyone again.

Three

———

Various changes had occurred in ICU by the time Elise reported for duty two days later. There were several new patients and Damon Trent was off the respirator. His face looked much better when she went in that afternoon to check him, although there was considerable bruising on his forehead and around his eyes.

"Good afternoon, Mr. Trent. I'm pleased to find you doing so well today."

He had been lying there, his hand restlessly brushing across the covers when she walked in.

She was back. The same voice, the same light scent, and yes, the same soft touch as she placed her fingers on his wrist.

"What is your name?" he said, his voice husky from nonuse.

Startled by the question and the fact that he could now speak, Elise hesitated for a moment. "Elise Brandon."

"Elise. That's a pretty name."

She smiled. "Thank you."

"What do you look like?"

She wondered if all the nurses who cared for him had been interrogated. Of course it must be such a helpless feeling to lie there and not be able to see all the people coming in and out of the room. "I'm tall, with light brown hair, green eyes, the regular number of ears and nose."

"How tall?"

"Tall. Five eight."

"How much do you weigh?"

"Are you serious? What difference does it make?"

"I'm trying to get a picture of you in my mind."

"Oh. Well, I weigh around 130 pounds, give or take a pound or two."

"So you're slender."

"I suppose."

"How long have you been a nurse?"

"Six years."

"Do you like it?"

"Very much."

"Are you married?"

"Now that, Mr. Trent, is absolutely none of your business."

He smiled. "I know. But I'm curious."

"A little curiosity never hurt a soul. You stay curious while I check these dressings."

"You aren't going to tell me."

"You got it."

"Why not?"

"Why should I?"

"Because I want to know."

"Do you always get your own way?"

"If I can possibly manage it."

"What you need is to build a little character by being denied a few things. It really is none of your business, you know."

"How old are you?"

"Old enough."

"Late twenties—early thirties?"

"Close."

"Then you're married."

"Whatever you say."

"Someone who looks like you and sounds like you would not be single for long."

"Sounds good, anyway."

"You aren't going to tell me."

She laughed. "You certainly are persistent, Mr. Trent."

"Damon. Please call me Damon. May I call you Elise?"

"I have a strong hunch it doesn't matter how I respond, you're going to call me what you wish."

"See how well we're getting to know each other already?" Although his smile was weak, it was still devastating. This man was high-powered in more than just business. Elise was actually glad he couldn't see her reaction to his teasing.

Of course that's all it was. He was bored, now that he was feeling somewhat better. She patted his hand. "If you need me, just push that button by your pillow." She started to leave the room.

"What if I need you now?"

She glanced around to see what she had forgotten to do. "What do you need?"

"Your company."

"Sorry, but you aren't my only patient. What if I have Mr. Drake come in?"

"Is he still here?"

"Yes, he came in about the time I came on duty."

"Yes, I'd like to see him."

She smiled, noting the brightening effect the idea of company had on him. Obviously Damon Trent was beginning to feel better.

"Hello, Damon."

"Justin, glad you're here. Did you get in touch with McCallahan?"

"Yes. I canceled the meeting in Miami for next week. He said there was no rush and I figured you would prefer to handle it."

"I told you to go ahead with it."

"I know, but I don't think McCallahan was interested in dealing with anyone but you."

"Then he may have a long wait."

"Do you know how much longer you're going to be in here?"

"Are you kidding? These people won't even let me know the time of day. By the way, what can you tell me about Elise Brandon?"

"The nurse?"

"Yes."

"I don't know. She seems very competent."

"No, I don't mean that. What does she look like?"

"Oho. Even flat on your back, you manage to notice the attractive females."

"Is she attractive?"

"Very."

"Describe her."

"She comes to about my shoulder, has beautiful eyes that tilt at the edge, which give her sort of an exotic look...if you know what I mean...high cheekbones, and a slight dent in her chin that's very attractive."

"I suppose you've already made a move in that direction."

"Are you kidding? Sexy nurses are the last thing I've had on my mind since you landed in here."

"So she's sexy, huh?"

"As a matter of fact, I'd say so. She has a cool aloofness about her that I find appealing."

"How does she wear her hair?"

"It's pulled back into some kind of knot on her neck, but instead of looking severe it frames her face, gives her almost a Madonna-like appearance." He paused. "The original Madonna, not the singer."

"Is she married?"

"I don't know. Why don't you ask her?"

"I did, but it didn't get me anywhere."

Justin started laughing. "Losing your touch, old man? I wish I'd been there to watch. So she put you in your place?"

"Something like that."

"And now you want me to find out more about her."

"Yes."

"How much more?"

"Everything you can find out."

Justin smiled. "I'll see what I can do. Now, then, what do you want me to do about Cynthia?"

"Don't tell me she's still here?"

"Not in the hospital, no. The doctor sat her down the other night and had a long talk about visitors and not upsetting you, and she has agreed to wait in her hotel until you're ready to see her."

"The bitch."

"The bitch has been your constant companion for a couple of months now."

"I know. I never claimed to have great taste in women."

"Until now."

"What's that supposed to mean?"

"The nurse seems to have considerable class and you're interested in her."

"Not in the same way. I'm just curious about her, wonder what makes her tick."

"That's what I mean. You never show that sort of interest in the women you usually see."

"So I'm bored."

"I'll send Cynthia over."

"No way. I can't believe she was trying to pass herself off as my fiancée. She knew better than that."

"Maybe that's the only way she thought she could get in to see you—as family."

"It won't work. Did she think you told everyone you were my brother, for God's sake? Tell her I still can't see anyone so she might as well get back to Chicago. I'll call her when I feel up to company."

"I'll try, but I'm not sure she'll buy it."

Damon sighed. The little energy he'd already exerted had depleted his slight reserve. "Why don't you see how soon they're going to let me out of here?"

"Probably not until you can go under your own steam. You're lucky to be alive, you know."

"I'm well aware of that. Every muscle and bone in my body has been letting me know just how alive I am. I'll be glad when my head quits aching."

"What did they say about your eyesight?"

"There was some talk about further tests and consultations. There's an eye specialist in New York who's flying in tomorrow. They have great hopes."

"How about you?"

"I'm taking one day at a time, Justin. It takes all the energy I can muster to do that."

"You're going to come out of this just fine, Damon. Nothing has ever been able to hold you back. This won't, either." He stood up. "Get some rest. I'll be back tomorrow."

"Find out if Elise Brandon is married."

"And if she is, am I supposed to do away with her husband?"

Damon chuckled. "Maybe that isn't such a bad idea at that."

"You're sick, you're really sick," Justin said, walking out the door.

No, just intrigued—by a touch, a tone, a scent and an illusion of someone special, someone he really wanted to get to know, if she'd let him.

With that thought, Damon drifted off to sleep.

As he slowly awakened, Damon Trent became aware of someone in his room. He felt so helpless, tied down with tubes and feedings and drains. He couldn't even sit up without help. For the past two days they'd had him sitting on the side of the bed—dangling, the damned nurse called it. It had taken all of his strength to sit upright. It unnerved him to recognize his own weakness. He didn't want to think about how long it would take him to build back his normal strength.

He caught a faint whiff of a scent, very fragile, almost like the ghost of a memory drifting across his mind.

"Elise?"

"I didn't mean to wake you," she responded softly.

"What time is it?"

"A little after ten."

"When do you go off duty?"

"Eleven."

"Have you been busy tonight?"

"Fairly."

"You haven't been in here very often." He heard the petulant tone and couldn't believe what he was hearing.

"Actually, I've been in every fifteen minutes or so, but you've been asleep. You need the rest. It aids your body in healing."

"I'm getting better, you know."

"Oh, yes. I see a marked improvement every day when I come to work."

"How much longer do you suppose I'll be here?"

"Getting bored with our accommodations?"

"Let's put it this way, there are several places I'd prefer to be right now."

He could hear the smile in her voice. "Name one."

"The lake."

"Which lake?"

"The Lake of the Ozarks. Don't tell me you've never been there."

"I wouldn't dream of it."

"Surely you've heard of it."

"Yes."

"And you've never been there?"

"I generally take my vacations visiting my mother in Tennessee."

"And where does your husband take his vacation?" he asked smoothly.

She ignored the question. "So tell me about the Lake of the Ozarks."

"That's where I was going when I had my accident. That's where I'm hoping to go when I get out of here."

"Do you have a place there?"

"Um-hmm."

"Is it right on the lake?"

"Within a stone's throw."

"How long have you lived there?"

"I don't actually live there. I spend most of my time in Chicago...or Miami...or Dallas...or San Francisco." He sighed. "But when I can get away, I head for the lake. It's beautiful there."

"I'm sure it is."

"Why don't you come down for a visit when I get out?"

"That wouldn't be a very good idea."

"Why not?"

She laughed. "Believe me, by the time you get away from here, you aren't going to want to have any reminders of your visit."

"You'd be a very pleasant reminder, Elise."

"Thank you. I need to get back to work, Damon. Get some rest."

"Will you be here tomorrow?"

"Yes."

"Good," he murmured. She walked out of his room more than a little distracted.

He was probably that friendly to all of his nurses, so why was she taking his interest in her so personally? He was bored and she was one of his most regular contacts on this shift. She only wished she didn't find herself thinking of him at odd times of the day and night.

Perhaps it was because she had never met anyone like him before, nor had the chance to become so quietly intimate with such a person. He was no longer a high-powered businessman. His accident had reduced him to being another victim of suffering. To be honest she was surprised that he never complained about the pain—it had to be intense. He never asked for additional medication, even though the doctor had advised him not to suffer through the pain, that his suffering wasn't necessary.

Even in his weakest moments she had sensed within him a fight to survive, to persevere and to overcome the weakness that had temporarily struck him down. She had no doubt that it was merely temporary.

He didn't talk about his lack of sight. Any fears he had were well hidden from those around him. He dealt with life straight on, pulled no punches, and accepted no excuses.

He also had the respect and loyalty of Justin Drake, who appeared to be a good judge of character. She smiled. But then, what did she know about judging character? Her heart seemed to have little judgment at all, which was why she had accepted the fact that her emotions would never again take precedence over her intellect. Not ever. She knew what was good for her and what wasn't. Falling in love with anyone was definitely a bad move and one she didn't intend to make.

Elise picked up Damon's chart and began to register her most recent findings.

Four

"Mr. Trent was put on a respirator about eleven this morning," the nurse going off duty reported to Elise when she came to work.

Elise felt the sudden spurt of adrenaline hit her system at the news. "What happened?"

"To be honest, I don't think the doctor knows. He said Mr. Trent took the news about his eyesight very well, but within fifteen minutes his vital signs started wavering and he went into shock."

"What was the outcome of the tests on his eyes?"

"The eye surgeon said that he wouldn't be able to operate for several months. And the odds aren't in Mr. Trent's favor that he'll regain his sight."

"Oh, no." Elise realized at that moment how much she had been identifying with all that Damon Trent had been experiencing. How was he going to handle this new development? Obviously his body was reacting to the new stress.

The day nurse updated her on the status of the other patient in her charge, and finally Elise found herself free to go check on Damon.

The shades were drawn, even though light or lack of it was not his problem. She quietly approached the side of his bed. He looked so still, and so drained. Seeing him back on the respirator forced her to realize how much she had counted on his continued improvement.

She remembered his teasing, his voice low and husky. She picked up his hand and gently stroked it. "Don't let this get you down, Damon," she whispered. "You're a fighter. I know you can come out of this even stronger." Her fingers lightly stroked across the frown lines in his forehead. "You'll get your eyesight back. I know you will. It will take some time for you to heal first, but you can use the time resting. You don't have to work *all* the time, you know."

His fingers stirred in her hand and she was comforted. She hoped he had heard her. Elise took her time checking his IVs and dressings. His surgical wound was healing nicely.

Had Justin Drake been there that day? she wondered, deciding to check Damon's chart to see if anyone had thought to contact Justin.

No notation had been made and she decided to try his motel. After letting the phone in his room ring several times she left her name and the hospital number for him to call when he came in.

At odd moments during the next few hours Elise found herself back in Damon's room, watching him, checking the monitor and the respirator, wanting to do something for him— give him strength, or comfort or the desire to fight once again. He lay there so still, as though the vital life spark within him had dimmed.

"Can you hear me, Damon?" she whispered just before she went off her shift. "I'm going home now. When I come back tomorrow I want to see you feeling better, do you understand me? I want to see that sexy smile of yours greeting me. I want you badgering me about my personal life.'' She lifted his hand and softly placed her lips against his palm. ''I want you well again. I know you can do it. Keep fighting.''

Elise was glad no one saw her when she came out of his room. The tears in her eyes were not in the least professional.

The phone was ringing when she let herself into her apartment and she sounded rather breathless when she finally managed to say, ''H'lo.''

''Elise?'' An unfamiliar male voice asked.

''Yes?''

''This is Justin Drake. I just got back into town and found your message, but the hospital said you'd already left. I hope you don't mind my calling you at home.''

''No, that's all right. They could have given you the same message I have.''

''Has something happened to Damon?'' The tight anxiety in his voice was evident.

''He's had something of a setback and I wasn't sure if anyone had notified you.''

"I've been in Chicago all day, trying to make sure things are running smoothly. What's happened?"

"The eye surgeon examined Damon today. He said he wouldn't consider surgery for several months. I'm afraid the news set Damon back physically as well as emotionally."

"Oh, God," Justin responded with a sigh. "That's really tough."

"Yes, it is. They put him back on the respirator earlier today, and he seemed to be resting more comfortably when I left this evening than he was when I first went on duty."

"I'll be up to see him first thing tomorrow."

"I'm sure he'd appreciate it."

"And I really appreciate your calling to let me know."

"I told you I would."

"Yes. You're definitely a woman of your word." He paused, wanting to comment on how much her care and attitude had helped Damon to get this far, but he wasn't sure that Damon would want her to know about his feelings. Justin wasn't even sure Damon had faced how attached he'd become to his evening nurse. He would do better not to say anything.

Justin recognized that the pause had become awkward. "Well, I'll let you go and probably see you tomorrow. Thanks again, Elise."

"You're welcome."

Elise put the phone down and wandered into the kitchen, trying to decide if she wanted to eat something before going to bed. She still felt too on edge to sit down and she found herself pacing in front of the cabinets, wondering if there were anything else she could do.

He seemed so alone in the world. Except for Justin, and the glamorous Cynthia, whom Elise hadn't seen in days, no one seemed interested in Damon and his recovery. The morning nurse had told her that several reporters showed up shortly after the accident to find out what they could. The doctor had talked with them but had not allowed any of them to visit Damon.

Eventually, Elise forced herself to eat a bowl of soup and part of a sandwich, then went on to bed where she lay for hours, unable to sleep. What was it about Damon that made him so memorable? Whatever it was, it had a damaging effect on her peace of mind.

As soon as Elise walked into his room the next afternoon Damon picked up pencil and paper, wrote something, then held it up to her. She read, "Where have you been?" and smiled. The strong, masculine strokes looked full of health and vitality, and she was greatly encouraged. Almost as encouraged as she was by the arrogant question.

"I'm glad to see you're awake, Damon. You must be feeling better."

He waved the clipboard.

"I've been right here. I just came on about fifteen minutes ago. There are a few procedures that need to be completed before I can check on you."

He wrote something else. "Where were you yesterday?"

"Oho. We're talking about yesterday. As a matter of fact, I was right here most of the afternoon, fussing around you, trying to make you comfortable, making sure everything was functioning normally. While you, my friend, managed to sleep through it."

He lowered the clipboard and pencil and wearily closed his eyes. Their keen gaze had lanced her with their silver-gray brilliance and her heart ached with the knowledge that he had no use of them.

She placed her hand on his wrist. His pulse rate had slowed considerably. She checked his temperature and was heartened to discover it was normal. He took her hand and squeezed it.

"I'm glad to see you're feeling well enough to flirt with the nurse," she teased, a little breathless at her own reaction.

He fumbled for the pad and wrote, "I hardly think hand holding can be considered flirting."

"Oh, I don't know. I would say it shows a certain amount of originality, considering you're flat on your back and barely able to move."

She missed his husky voice and a lump formed in her throat. She could only hope that by tomorrow he would be taken off the respirator once more.

Justin Drake walked into the room two days later and smiled. Damon was sitting on the side of the bed, a young nurse holding him in order to help him keep his balance. Once again he was off the respirator and seemed to be recovering rapidly from his recent setback.

"Good morning, boss. Thought I'd better check in."

Damon raised his head, his eyes gazing toward Justin. "How are things?"

"Simmering. Nothing has boiled over, but a few items need your personal touch to turn them into masterpieces."

Damon smiled. "It's nice to be needed."

"Don't ever doubt it, my friend." He shook hands with the older man, then sat down in the only chair in the room.

"I think that's long enough for today, Mr. Trent," the young nurse said. Justin watched as Damon gratefully stretched out on the bed once more. He was still very weak, but his color was much better than it had been. He was looking more like the preaccident Damon.

"I'm surprised you haven't decided to grow a beard while you're laid up in here," Justin offered.

Damon chuckled. "Not with these nurses. They've insisted on shaving me every morning before I'm even properly awake."

The nurse smiled at Justin, then spoke to Damon. "The doctor said that we can start feeding you clear liquids today if you'd like."

Damon's brow lifted slightly. "Lucky me." To Justin he offered, "Now I can offer to share a meal with you. Before, you would have had to bring your own tube."

Once the nurse left, Justin leaned forward and said, "It looks like you're going to make it out of here in no time."

Damon nodded. "You know, I had the weirdest experience a few days ago. I've had it on my mind and wasn't at all sure I wanted to mention it to anyone, for fear they'd think my mind was going."

"What happened?"

"It was the day I found out about my eyes. I must have gone downhill after that. I don't remember. That's why this is so strange. I don't remember that day at all. What I do remember is struggling through a black, heavy fog, trying to find my way out. I had almost decided to forget about it and was looking for a place to rest when I heard a voice—Elise's voice. She was calling to me, as though I were a child late to supper. She called and called, sometimes loudly, sometimes sounding angry.

Other times it was as though she were crying, but she kept telling me to come on. I remember being irritated that she wouldn't leave me alone. I was so tired and I'd been struggling for so long. But I started following her voice and the closer I seemed to get, the lighter everything seemed around me. Then it seemed like I was out in the sunshine. I can remember the light hurt my eyes, but I could see. Only she wasn't there."

Both men were silent. The quiet, steady beep of the monitor was the only sound in the room and Justin sat there, studying the man he'd known for years in a professional sense, but had only recently begun to know on a personal basis.

Damon Trent was a very private man. He never talked about his family. All Justin knew was what he'd heard. That Damon had once been married, but that his wife had died of a congenital heart condition several years earlier. There had never been mention of children, or parents or anyone else.

Justin wondered what Elise represented to Damon. He had never seen her. Perhaps he would be disappointed if he ever did. Right now he could allow his imagination to run free and she could be whatever he wanted or needed her to be in his life—a friend, confidante, lover, wife.

What happened to a person who was critically ill? What sort of fantasies did they harbor?

"I suppose you think I've really gone around the bend," Damon finally offered, almost apologetically.

"Not at all. As a matter of fact, I was thinking how accurate your assessment of Elise is, even though you've never seen her. It was Elise who contacted me that day to let me know you'd had a setback."

"Oh?"

"I didn't get her message until after she'd gone off duty, so I called her at her home. She seemed truly concerned about you."

Damon considered that for a while. "It's strange, the bond that can occur between a patient and the staff. I'm utterly dependent on them, and I resent them for it, except for Elise. For some reason she doesn't make me feel helpless. She teases me, jokes with me and makes me feel capable of walking out of here."

"Which you're bound to do shortly."

"The question is when."

"First things first. You eat your liquids and eventually they'll feed you vegetables. You get that licked, and just maybe we can get you out of here."

"Vegetables?" he scoffed. "I can't think of better encouragement than that."

"Will it help your speedy recovery to learn that Elise Brandon is no longer married?"

"No longer?"

"That's right. She and Guy Brandon were married eight years ago; divorced six months ago."

"Did you find out anything about him?"

"That he's good looking, makes money, is very charming and can't seem to leave the women alone. I understand that was what caused the divorce."

"It doesn't make much sense. Unless all of my senses are betraying me, I can't understand someone being married to Elise Brandon and looking at anyone else."

"I don't think he had to look. In his business it was generally offered to him. He owns a travel agency here in town and goes on many of the tours himself. He has a wonderful gift of gab, marvelous sense of humor, or so the young woman who was so willing to share all of this with me confided, and never wanted to hurt a woman's feelings by telling her no.''

Damon laughed. ''The man is all heart.''

''That's what I thought. None of that charm hurt his career any, either. He was particularly persuasive with the older women, who responded to his flattery and lovemaking by booking tours with him for themselves and all of their friends.''

''And Elise got tired of it?''

''I got the impression she was unaware of what he was doing. He had a real flair for telling the convincing lie. I suppose she loved him enough to buy his stories.''

''How did she find out?''

''One of his lies caught up with him ... and one of his little playmates took him a little more seriously than he bargained for. The end result was that Elise moved out, his playmate moved in, Elise filed and obtained a divorce. End of story.''

''It happens all the time.''

''I know. Still, it's a shame it had to happen to Elise. According to friends, she was a one-man woman and Guy was it. He never appreciated what he had, from all accounts. She's a real class act.''

"His loss is my gain."

"What do you mean by that? Surely you aren't going to start courting her from a sickbed."

"I'm going to court her any way I can. At least now I understand what I'm up against. As friendly as she is, she won't discuss anything of a personal nature. Now I know not to push."

"How do you intend to conduct this romance?"

"With carefully planned strategy. How else?"

"Of course. Is it all right, O mighty leader, if I sit back and take notes?"

"Very funny."

"Would you like me to put in a good word or two for you? Try to convince her of your sterling qualities?"

"Why do I get the feeling you're amused?"

"Because you're talking about forming a relationship with a woman in the same manner you form business relationships—find out everything you can about them, positive and negative, discover weak points, spend time with them, then make your move."

"What's wrong with that?"

"Maybe nothing. That's why I've decided to hide and watch. I have a feeling the next few weeks are going to be very interesting."

Five

During the weeks that followed Elise looked forward to going to work each day, just to discover what outrageous thing Damon would say to her. At least he no longer pushed her for personal details, for which she was grateful. Somehow she felt the less he knew about her life outside the hospital, the safer she was from him. Why she needed to feel safe, she wasn't sure.

Some evenings when it was quiet she would sit in his room and talk with him—about music, or books or the latest trend in entertain-

ment. He shared with her some of the business
negotiations his company was presently involved in, and explained why Justin was unable to be there to visit—he was busy traveling
between Chicago and Miami, the site of Damon's latest acquisition.

Elise asked questions, wondering what mo-
tivated him. Was it the quest for power, then
more power? Money, then more money? What
created the drive within him? Amazingly
enough, he was candid with her, giving her
questions serious thought. Sometimes he had
to admit that he didn't know the answer. No
one had ever asked him the question, nor had
he ever asked himself.

Elise pretended she wasn't getting involved
with him, wasn't treating him any differently
than she would any other patient who had
been in critical condition, with so many problems to overcome. She pretended that she
didn't find him fascinating, tried to hide the
fact that his quick wit and piercing intellect
stimulated her.

Elise was handling everything very well—
until the afternoon she came to work and
found his room occupied by someone else.

"Where's Mr. Trent?" she asked Diana.

"Oh, we moved him to the surgical floor this morning. The doctor is quite pleased with his progress."

Elise felt a heavy lump form in her chest. Of course she was glad he was better, but she recognized how much she would miss him. After being in the hospital for almost two months, he no longer needed the specialized nursing offered in intensive care.

She kept herself busy all afternoon with her new patient, forcing her attention away from thoughts of Damon. He was no longer a part of her life, even professionally, but she felt very grateful to have gotten to know him.

On her way back from supper she absently noted she still had about ten minutes before she needed to relieve the other nurse. She stopped at the nurses' desk on the surgical floor.

"What room is Damon Trent in?"

A young redheaded nurse smiled. "He's in 316. Isn't he something? The whole floor was atwitter when they moved him here today."

"Do you know if he has any visitors?"

"I don't think so. No one has asked for him."

Elise quietly walked down the hallway and paused before room 316. She was trembling. *Perhaps he's asleep. If so, I won't wake him.* Quietly she pushed open the door and peered inside the room.

Damon turned his head toward the door, his move alert. "Elise? Is that you?"

Her heart tumbled in her chest and she caught her breath. "How did you know?"

He smiled. "I always know when it's you. Come on in. I appreciate your coming to see me."

Hesitantly she walked over to the side of the bed. "Have you had any company today?"

"You're the first."

"Is Justin still out of town?"

"Yes, although now he plans to call me each day and report in."

"I suppose you're getting a little bored."

"You could say that. Why, were you thinking about bringing me some toy soldiers to play with?"

"What a great idea."

"Forget it." He reached out toward her and without thinking she took his hand. "I missed you today."

How could she admit that she had missed him, too?

"Do you suppose you could stop in to see me once in a while?"

"Perhaps," she said noncommittally.

Damon gently lifted her hand to his lips and placed a soft kiss on her knuckles. "Thank you."

Her heart thundered so in her chest she was certain he could hear it. He had never treated her this way before. He had always been casual and friendly. Now he was almost loverlike. Quite frankly, Elise didn't know how to handle it.

As a rule, she had no problem dealing with amorous patients, but Damon was different because she had taken the time to get to know him. They had become friends.

During the time she had spent with him, she had never once heard him complain about his injuries, the possibility of permanent blindness, or show any negativity to the cards life had recently dealt him. She admired this man more than she could possibly put into words, more than she had actually acknowledged to herself. How could she be rude to him at this point? The answer was, she couldn't.

So she didn't say anything.

"I've embarrassed you, haven't I?" he murmured. "I'm sorry. I didn't mean to do that." He attempted to smile. "Could it be that I've been listening to too many soaps on television?"

Since she knew very well he hadn't been watching television—in fact, there had not been one in either of his rooms—she recognized his attempt to lighten the atmosphere.

She searched for something equally light to say. "I imagine that could prove interesting—just listening to the sounds of a soap. What do you hear? A lot of heavy breathing and sighs?"

He grinned. "Something like that. I've always wondered how people could keep track of the many different characters and story lines. It's even tougher when you can't see them, but can only go by their voices."

She laughed, just as he meant for her to do. "Is that how you recognize me, by my voice?"

"Among other things. I seem to have this extra sense where you're concerned." *Whoa, that wasn't going to help lighten the conversation.* He felt her hand tense and he obligingly released it.

"I have to go now. My supper break is over."

"Thank you for coming by."

"If you'd like, I'll stop by before I report to work tomorrow."

He heard the hesitancy, the shyness, and was heartened by it. If he didn't rush her, perhaps he could coax her to him. He certainly wasn't in any condition to do any chasing, that was for sure.

Long after Elise had left, Damon still thought about her. He played devil's advocate, questioning his interest in her, pointing out his state of boredom, and the fact that she had been there when he was in so much pain. Probably as soon as he was mobile, he would lose interest.

Let's face it, I've never been that interested in a woman for her conversation before.

Not since Kathleen had died had Damon felt the tenderness that seemed to overcome him whenever Elise was near. Kathleen had been very special—a gift from his childhood that he had nurtured until she was gone. The women he knew now were sophisticated and offered him companionship and comfort. In return he offered them a good time, expensive presents and an entrée into his world of money and power. A fair exchange, or so it had seemed until now.

What did he want from Elise? How could a woman's voice affect him so, create such a longing deep inside, stir up feelings that he had never had for another woman, not even Kathleen—his wife?

For God's sake, I've never even seen her. But Justin has, he reminded himself. *So what? We've never been attracted to the same women before. Justin didn't say he was attracted, did he? But he likes her. I can tell by his tone of voice when he speaks of her.* He wondered if his hospital stay was creating jealousy of his own assistant.

He was going to have to find something to occupy his mind. If only they would let him get out of there. First thing in the morning he was going to pin the doctor down and find out the very earliest he could leave. What was being done for him now that couldn't be done down at the lake? He was eating a regular diet. He was off the damned machines.

The more he thought about it, the more he was convinced he should be able to go home—and soon.

* * *

"Ah, there you are," Damon said with a wide smile before Elise had a chance to walk over to him.

"How do you do that?" she asked with exasperation.

"I have a homing device planted on you that gives off a signal whenever you're near," he explained with a straight face.

"And just how did you manage to place that homing device on me?"

"A secret in the industry. Can't give secrets away, you know."

"I'm glad to see you looking so pleased with yourself," she offered.

"I've got a proposition for you."

Her heart started behaving erratically and Elise gave a quick thanks that she wasn't hooked up to a monitor.

He chuckled at her silence. "What a suspicious mind you have. I wasn't talking about that sort of proposition."

"I suppose now you're going to tell me your secret homing device also reads minds."

"No, it's just that I've gotten well enough acquainted with you to know you have a very suspicious mind. And you're wrong."

"What is your proposition?"

"I want you to come home with me."

"And I'm not supposed to be suspicious of that offer?"

"Not at all. I want you in your professional capacity. I talked with the doctor today and he's seriously considering releasing me if I have competent nursing care at home. I'd like you to be the competent nurse. How about it?"

For just a moment she actually allowed herself to consider it. Damon had spent quiet hours describing the lake and how he felt whenever he was there—the peacefulness, the tranquillity, the sunlight and glinting water. Then she shook her head. *Quit dreaming*.

"This may come as a shock to you, Mr. Trent, but I have a job that requires my presence five days a week from three to eleven each evening."

"But don't you have any time coming?"

"Not really."

"Couldn't you ask for a leave of absence?"

"I could. But I don't intend to. I'm sure you can find any number of special duty nurses who will be able to assist you." She stood up.

He fumbled for her hand and urged her nearer to the bed. In a soft, husky voice, he said, "But I want you."

How dare he turn on the charm! Couldn't he understand *no* when he heard it? Elise could feel her anger build. She had little tolerance left for the typical charming male who insisted on getting his own way.

"It sounds as though you need to do some more character building, Damon. You're getting a little demanding, aren't you?"

The quick flash of hurt across his face surprised her. She hadn't meant to allow her anger to show, and she certainly didn't intend to hurt him, but he was pushing, and she had made up her mind that no one would ever coerce her by playing on her emotions. No one.

"I've got to go to work," she said, pulling her hand out of his.

He nodded, his face carefully blank.

Damn him, it's all I can do to keep myself from apologizing to him! Elise left the room, determined not to come back, determined not to pit her meager strength against the charm and charisma of another attractive male.

Unfortunately for Elise's firm resolve, circumstances seemed to be working against her.

The first small crumbling of her resistance
came as a result of a phone call she received
that afternoon from her mother.

"Elise, dear, I'm sorry to call you at work
but I was afraid I might miss you if I tried to
reach you at home."

"That's all right, Mom. Is something
wrong?"

"Oh, no! On the contrary, I have some
marvelous news."

"What's that?"

"Melanie and I have been invited to go with
Joe and Beverly to Italy."

Melanie was Elise's eighteen-year-old sister
and Joe was her mother's brother. "Why,
Mom, that's wonderful."

"Isn't it, though? Mel and I are so excited
we're both reduced to babbling incoherently to
each other. The thing is, they've scheduled the
trip for the month of August and that's when
you were planning to come down to visit."

"That certainly isn't a problem. I can always reschedule my trip."

"I know you can. I just feel like we're running out on you. I know how you look forward to coming down here to relax. Perhaps
you can plan to go somewhere else this year. A

change in your routine might be just what you need."

Elise thought of Damon's offer. Being with him at the lake would certainly be a shift in her routine but she wasn't sure she was ready for such a drastic change.

"Don't worry about me, Mom. You and Mel go and have a good time. I expect to receive all kinds of colorful postcards and descriptions. You may want to import one of those Italian playboys for me."

"What would you do with him if I did?"

"Oh, I'd try to figure out something. You need to have more faith in my imaginative abilities."

Her mother laughed. "I'll let you get back to work, then. We'll talk again before we leave."

"Tell Melanie not to break too many hearts while she's over there." Elise was very proud of her little sister.

So now I don't have plans for my vacation, Elise realized as she hung up. She dismissed the thought from her mind and went back to work.

Later that day on her way to the cafeteria for supper, she met Justin Drake in the hall. She smiled and would have walked past him except that he stopped and spoke.

"I was going down to ICU to see you," he said.

"To see me?" she asked, puzzled.

"Yes. I was wondering if I could talk with you for a moment."

"I'm going to supper but you're welcome to come with me, if you'd like. We only take forty minutes for supper as a rule."

Justin walked beside her, matching his long stride to hers. "Have you seen Damon today?"

"No."

He was silent and she wondered why he had asked. Was Damon wondering why she hadn't come to see him? "How is he?"

"The doctor says he's progressing satisfactorily, and I suppose that should be good enough."

"But it isn't enough for you or him, is that it?"

"You have to understand Damon. He's a very active person, on the go constantly. He's a mover and a shaker and this thing has been a blow to him in more than the physical sense." Justin held a swinging door open for

Elise, then followed her. "Damon isn't used to inaction. He isn't used to waiting for things to happen. He generally makes things happen."

"I'm sure it's hard for him. No one really enjoys being a patient."

"I've talked with his doctor to see if I could take him out of here, but he explained he has several weeks of convalescing to do before he can be on his own again."

"Yes, the body works miracles in rehabilitating itself, but needs the time to do it."

"The doctor did say that Damon could be released much sooner if he had someone—a nurse—to look after him for a few weeks at home."

They had reached the cafeteria and Justin handed Elise a tray, then took one for himself. They went through the line in silence, Elise already understanding why Justin wanted to talk with her. If Damon couldn't get results on his own, then he would send his number-one henchman to coerce her. Elise found Damon's arrogance offensive.

After they'd placed their dishes on one of the vacant tables and sat down opposite each other, Justin spoke again.

"Damon mentioned to me that he asked you to be that nurse and that you said no."

She met his gaze with an unwavering stare. "That's correct."

"Would I be out of line asking why you don't want to take the job?"

"Because I already have a job and that position calls for a special duty nurse."

"But it wouldn't be a full-time position. You could consider it a vacation with extra pay. You'd have plenty of time to rest and enjoy yourself while you were there as well as receiving a good salary."

Elise didn't say anything. Instead, she continued to eat.

"I checked with your supervisor and found out you have three weeks' accumulated vacation if you wanted to take some time off from the hospital."

Her green eyes had darkened with anger. "You can tell Mr. Trent that I meant what I said. He didn't need to send you to try to convince me. Believe me, his powers of persuasion were quite adequate without your adding yours to them."

Justin stared at her in surprise. "You think Damon asked me to speak with you?"

"Didn't he?"

"No. He told me he'd asked you, you said no, and for me to find out how he could hire a special duty nurse, which was why I was talking with the nurse supervisor." He paused to take a sip of his coffee. "As a matter of fact, Damon would be irritated to learn I was pleading his case. He has an overabundance of pride."

"And arrogance," she muttered.

"I thought you had gotten to know him better than that. Damon allowed you to see a side of him that few people even know exist. I'd worked for him for almost five years before he unbent enough around me to let me see his human side."

"It's hard to carry emotional shields when you're as ill as Damon was."

"Well, for what it's worth, you should feel gratified to know you got past all of his defenses."

"What's that supposed to mean?"

"It means that for the first time since his wife died, Damon is showing a real interest in a woman."

"What about Cynthia Rydell?"

"I said an interest. Cynthia was a convenience. They had a mutually satisfying relationship where neither expected more than the other was willing to give. That's not what he has with you."

"He has nothing with me. Nothing at all."

"Is that position comfortable?"

"What are you talking about?"

"You. Burying your head in the sand in that manner would seem to be a very uncomfortable position."

"All right. So I was concerned about Damon. I care about all of my patients. But he's no longer my patient."

"No. Now he wants to be your friend, have the opportunity to get to know you better. What's wrong with that?"

"There's no reason for a friendship to develop between the two of us."

"Isn't there?"

She forced herself to meet his gaze but the tiny glow of sympathy she saw there unnerved her. He certainly had no reason to feel sorry for her! "No. We live in separate worlds and there's no reason to think we'll ever see each other again."

"Interesting you should use that phrase since it might be Damon who'll never see anyone again. But he's not dwelling on it, not using it to gain sympathy."

She thought of Damon and the way he had looked the last time she had seen him—that flash of hurt when she had been so curt with him. She thought of his courage and recognized how little courage she had anymore. She was afraid of being hurt, afraid of becoming too attached to someone, so that she was crawling into an emotional hole and refusing to come out.

Justin was quiet, as though he'd said all he was going to say on the subject. She finished her meal in silence.

Finally she glanced up at him. "I'm not saying I'll do it. But I'll give it some more thought. May I give you an answer in a few days?"

"I may not be here. Why don't you tell Damon?"

The thought of facing Damon again gave her shivers. Why did she react to him so? She didn't like it at all, this feeling of not being in control of her emotions. Too many long days and nights of struggling to overcome pain and resentment had gone into her present state of accepting her life. She had no desire for anyone to come along and make waves in her hard-earned serenity.

Six

Elise spent an uneasy night wrestling with her choices. She finally admitted to herself that there was nothing she wanted to do as much as she wanted to accept Damon's offer. Damon fascinated her. Quite frankly, she'd never known another man like him. And he had shown definite interest in getting to know her better as well. So what was wrong with taking her vacation time and going to the lake with him?

For the first time in her life Elise forced herself to face her fears—fear of rejection, fear of being hurt again, fear of failure. When she finally drifted off to sleep her dreams were filled with the terrors of uncertainty and of the unknown. When she awoke the next day, nothing had been resolved. Her fear had immobilized her.

Consequently—her life seemed to have a way of making her face whatever it was she was running away from—she was almost prepared for the news that awaited her when she arrived at the hospital for work.

"We only have two patients in ICU today," she was informed by the supervisor of the ward. "Surgical is really crowded, so you'll be working there today."

With a certain amount of calm resignation Elise accepted the news that she would be working on Damon's floor. Later she wasn't even surprised to find he was one of her assigned patients. Ready or not, she was going to be forced to deal with her attraction to him and her fear of that attraction.

He was asleep when she entered his room and stood by his side, quietly studying him. His color was much improved from the last time she'd seen him, although his tan had definitely faded. The stitches on his forehead were healing nicely and the frown lines between his brows were almost gone—a sign that the pain he'd been experiencing was lessening.

Damon appeared relaxed in his sleep as though he had mentally willed himself to accept his limitations of the moment and to allow his body time to heal.

Elise had a strong desire to smooth his dark hair off his forehead and to press a kiss against his cheek. She mentally shook herself, reminding herself of her need for objectivity and professionalism. How quickly her attachment to him had grown.

One of the first things she had learned as a nurse was not to become emotionally involved with the patients, and yet she was forced to acknowledge that she was very much involved with this man. She admired so much about him and wanted to learn more. Would he regain his eyesight? If not, what changes would occur in his life and how would he handle those changes?

Elise knew enough about him to know he would face life with a great deal of courage and determination. Perhaps one of the reasons she was drawn to him was her recognition that she lacked both courage and determination in her life. Wasn't it oftentimes the case—that one was most attracted to traits that one lacked?

Damon's eyes suddenly opened. "Elise?" he said, his voice husky.

"Yes."

He smiled slightly. "I was dreaming about you. How long have you been here?"

"Just a few minutes."

"Have you forgiven me for upsetting you?"

It was her turn to smile. "There was nothing to forgive."

"I'm glad you came back. I've missed you."

She wanted to tell him how much she had missed him as well. But she didn't. "I'm working this floor today since ICU isn't busy."

A flash of disappointment flitted across his face, then was gone. "Oh."

"But I had intended to come see you anyway," she hastily explained, wanting the warmth in his face to return. Then she heard herself saying, "If you haven't found a nurse to go to the lake, I'm willing to spend three weeks with you, if that will help."

When had she made up her mind to go? When she saw him again? When she faced how very much she wanted to be around him? She

didn't know—would probably never know—
and it no longer mattered.

What mattered was the sudden brightening
of his face and the wide smile that appeared.
It was as though a bright light had been turned
on inside him, radiating throughout his body.
Could her continued presence really mean so
much to him? Elise could feel the heavy thudding of her heart in her chest. She had made
her commitment, fear or no fear, and she was
prepared to face the outcome.

"It's time for you to get up and walk." She
hurried into speech, trying to bring a normal
routine to their conversation, determined to
hold any personal feelings at bay.

Damon would have none of it. With her help
he sat up in bed and swung his long, pajama-
clad legs over the side of the bed. Pulling her
between his knees, he slipped his hands on either side of her face. "Thank you, Elise. I
know how hard a decision it must have been
for you."

His look of sympathy and understanding
unnerved her so that she was unaware of the
slight pressure he placed on her to move closer
to him, until she realized he was only inches
away from her. His lips unerringly found hers

and she stood motionless, shocked with the physical touch, because it felt so natural, so marvelously easy to stand there while his fingers softly explored the contours of her face and his mouth memorized hers.

Elise slowly slid her hands up his chest and around his neck, enjoying the feel of the muscles that his enforced convalescence had not destroyed.

Damon felt her relax in his arms and his heart quickened its steady rhythm. He wasn't sure where he'd found the nerve to attempt intimacy with her. For so long now she had been a part of his every waking and sleeping moment that it had seemed natural to him to express his joy at her intention to go to the lake with him by kissing her.

The scent of flowers surrounded him. Kissing her was like sipping nectar from a spring bouquet. Her lips were soft and pliable, slightly trembling, and he gently molded his mouth to hers, seeking to reassure her, enjoying the closeness, gaining even more determination that he would persist with this woman until she recognized that what they shared was something special, something not to be ignored. It was too late for either of them to walk away and pretend the relationship didn't exist.

Damon had to release her to catch his breath. His chest hurt with the need for more air and his heart thumped erratically in his chest.

Elise suddenly became aware that she was at work, kissing one of her patients. What if someone walked in? Whatever had she been thinking of? But of course she had not been thinking at all—she had been feeling. She had allowed her emotions to gain the upper hand for those few precious minutes.

Damon gave a soft chuckle. "You might want to wait a while before you check my pulse. It seems to have run away with itself." He stroked her cheek gently. "You seem to have that effect on me whenever you're around."

Elise hastily backed out of reach, then realized he needed her support to stand. She busily found his slippers and robe, silently helped him put them on and steadied him when he stood up.

"Did my kiss offend you?" he asked quietly.

She shook her head, too dazed to speak, then reminded herself he couldn't see her. "No, it didn't offend me," she murmured. "But it isn't a way I prefer to behave while on duty."

"I didn't mean to take advantage of the situation, Elise, please believe that. It was an impulse that I followed." She took his arm and guided him to the door. "I didn't mean to embarrass you."

She smiled. "You didn't, but I'd prefer to keep our relationship on a professional basis."

He turned his head in her direction at her words. Elise realized this was the first time she'd seen him on his feet. She hadn't realized how tall he was. Most of the men she knew were only an inch or two taller than she was. With Damon, she barely came to his chin.

"Even when we leave the hospital?"

Elise hesitated. How could she answer that truthfully? "I don't know," she finally answered.

"Thank you for your honesty. I'm hoping to convince you that our relationship can deepen without threat to your professional integrity."

She chuckled. "I think that's what I'm afraid of."

"Good. That will keep you off balance enough to give me a chance."

"A chance for what?"

"A chance to convince you that there's something between us that needs to be explored."

"I'm beginning to face that myself."

He patted her hand. "Then you've come a long way since the last time we talked."

Surprised at his perception and the unwitting changes going on inside her, she said, "Yes. Yes, I have."

They reached the end of the hallway and she guided him to turn around. They walked the length of the ward hallway several times in silence, Damon content with the progress he'd made with her, Elise recognizing the walls that had crumbled around her that day, unsure of how to start rebuilding. Did she need them at all? If so, did she need to keep Damon on the other side, or safe behind the walls with her?

The doctor was still not eager to release Damon, even with the knowledge that Elise would be with him. He discussed his concerns with her.

"Although his other injuries have been healing well, we're still dealing with an unknown where his eyes are concerned. What he needs most right now is rest and quiet. However, as he steadily improves, the confines of the hospital are causing him to become more and more restless, which could very well hinder his progress." He drummed his fingers on the chart he was holding. "It's hard to know where to draw the line. If he would go home and be quiet, allow his body and his nerves to heal, then I would say that is the answer. If, however, he uses his home as his office and gets involved with his work, it could be the worst thing for him." He studied Elise. "I see your role more as a psychological one. You need to keep him occupied and keep his mind off his work."

Elise could feel the heat rise in her face. In her mind was a vivid picture of how she could keep him distracted, and from the dancing light in the doctor's eyes, she was certain he recognized her thoughts.

"What would you suggest?" she asked, forcing herself to meet the amused expression in his eyes.

"See that he gets plenty of rest, try to shield him from unwelcome intrusions—you know the sort of things that would worry or upset him." He looked down at his notes. "Perhaps you could arrange with Mr. Drake that Damon's calls be screened, as well as his visitors." He grinned. "If he could see, I would suggest your wearing your most skimpy sunsuits. That should be distracting enough to anyone!"

"But would that be healthy for him?" she asked with an impudent smile.

He laughed. "The greatest therapy in the world, my dear. That sort of stress can be very stimulating."

"When are you going to release him?"

"Mr. Drake said he would be here on Friday. That's only two more days. I think it would make the transition easier for everyone if Mr. Drake were on hand to assist."

She nodded. "Fine. I'll clear the time with my supervisor and be ready to leave then."

"I'm pleased that you're going to be with him, Elise. I noticed his positive responses to you when he was so very ill. You have a powerful effect on him, one that is very rare to find.'' He patted her hand. ''I also think the change will do you good as well.''

She had known Damon's doctor for several years, but only in a professional capacity, and was a little startled at the personal turn of the conversation. ''I think so, too,'' she admitted shyly.

''If any problems arise, I want to be notified immediately.''

''Of course.''

''But I don't expect any. If I did, I wouldn't allow him to leave.''

''I know.''

''Keep in touch.'' He handed her the chart after making a few hieroglyphic notes, and strode down the hallway, a dedicated physician with a great deal of compassion. Elise had never before realized how much respect she had for him.

His comments made a great deal of sense.

For the next two days Elise had a keen feeling of anticipation as though one chapter of her life had been completed and another one was waiting to begin. She found herself smiling for no reason, remembering Damon's gentle teasing, and she knew that no matter what happened during the next three weeks, nothing in her life would ever be the same.

Elise stopped in to see Damon the evening before they were to leave. It was her last scheduled day to work and she was excited. She felt as though she were in truth going on vacation. Damon was sitting in a large leather chair beside his bed when she walked in.

"Good evening," she said, pushing open the door to his room and entering.

He glanced around, his face lighting up. "I wasn't sure if you were going to come see me tonight or not."

"I wasn't, either. My dinner hour kept getting pushed back. We've had several new cases admitted since I got here."

"Have you had a chance to eat?"

"After a fashion. The cafeteria was closed, but I was able to warm up a sandwich from a vending machine."

"Doesn't sound too appetizing."

She laughed. "That's the first thing you learn in this profession. Eat what you can when you can and don't quibble over quantity or quality. Otherwise, you'll spend your life grousing about the lousy hours and food."

"You don't spend much time complaining about anything, do you?"

"Oh, yes, I do. Don't try to make a saint out of me, Damon."

"I'd never think of it. Saint Elise has such an ethereal sound to it, not at all what I picture when I think of you."

"Thank you . . . I think."

"Oh, it was a compliment, you can be sure of that."

"I suppose you're all ready to spring this joint in the morning," she said with a slight drawl.

"Yes. Hospital life just isn't me."

She studied the man seated before her, the cool ice-blue of his silk pajamas reflected in the silver-gray of his eyes. It was hard to reconcile the picture of him now with the way he'd looked the first time she'd seen him. Considering the number and seriousness of his injuries, it was a wonder he had even lived. What had caused him to survive? She wondered what secret was locked deep within him that made him fight the odds—and win.

That secret strength called to her soul like a siren's voice. There was something within her that responded, causing her to identify with

that strength, and she felt a sense of yearning
to be nearer to him, to share in that strength
and determination.

"How long have you been up?"

He shrugged. "I have no idea."

"Are you tired?"

"A little."

"Would you like help getting back into bed,
or would you prefer to wait for the nurse on
duty?"

He grinned, a boyish, mischievous grin that
tugged at her heart. "I think I'd rather have
you help me."

Of course he didn't need help. He stood up
slowly and felt his way along the bed. She
stood within arm's reach but allowed him to
turn and sit down, watching while he kicked
off his shoes. Elise pulled the covers back so
that he could lie down but he remained sitting, looking in her direction expectantly.

"Don't I get a good-night kiss?" he asked
softly.

Elise was glad he couldn't see her face. It
would give so much away. She had been
thinking of the last kiss they had shared, recognizing that part of her anticipation of the
coming weeks was due to the opportunity to

share that closeness with him. It was almost as though he had read her mind.

He reached out and touched her, his hand sliding from her cheek down to her neck, then slipping just below her collar, cupping the tender area and slowly tightening his grip.

Mesmerized, Elise allowed herself to be drawn to him. She stared into the brightness of his eyes and when his other arm fastened around her waist, instead of feeling trapped she felt as though she'd found her home.

His kiss was no longer tentative or unsure. His mouth found hers like a homing device locked on target. Their mutual possession seemed to be asked for and acknowledged between them. His tongue gently outlined the shape of her mouth, then nudged gently for entry. Without conscious thought Elise complied with his nonverbal request so that he entered her mouth in a strong surge, taking her, possessing her, suddenly making her his.

His hold tightened and she seemed to flow against him, her softness meeting and melting against his strong, muscled chest. Her hands found the back of his head and restlessly explored the thick texture of his hair.

Damon reveled in the soft, sweet taste of her—his many dreams now being enacted—his senses filled with the scent of her, the essence of her, and he knew that this woman belonged to him. He'd never seen her, he might not ever see her, but her imprint was on his brain as surely as if his eyes had placed it there.

He felt the quivering of her body and knew that what they shared was new to her and she was wary of it. And why shouldn't she be? When he first recognized how differently he was reacting to this one person out of all the women he'd ever known, he'd been panicked as well. With his emotions so heavily involved, he no longer had complete control of what was happening to him.

But he had long since overcome the sense of unfamiliarity because he had recognized why she was so important to him. She was his other half, even though she might not as yet want to deal with the idea. It was up to him to show her, in simple stages, without rushing, how much they had to gain in pursuing a relationship.

His kiss told her of his desire for her, of his eagerness to possess her, to keep her in his life. Mindlessly Elise responded to his messages, allowing herself to feel the emotions he evoked within her.

She loved him. When she was alone once again she'd examine the knowledge and probably be panicked by the thought. But for now it was enough to be in his arms, enjoying his closeness and his expertise. His kiss demolished what little defenses she'd been able to build against him.

Elise was being forced to accept and deal with her own feelings for the man. Breathlessly she managed to pull away from him. "Is that your idea of a good-night kiss?" she managed to say, trying for lightness.

He let his hands slide sensuously along her body as he released her, then stretched out on the bed in front of her. "Let's just say I find it a nice way to end the evening before crawling into bed." A devilish grin lit up his face.

"It certainly didn't put me in a sleepy mood," she managed to say.

"Me, either."

She backed away from the bed. "I'll be back in the morning."

He nodded, satisfied that she had received his message. "Yes," he agreed. "You will. I'm looking forward to our time together."

Elise felt that every nerve in her body was standing up and shouting for release, for relief from the tension the kiss had caused. She felt branded, as though when she walked out of his room everyone who saw her would know that she was different now. She belonged to Damon Trent. How had he done it?

"Good night, Damon," she finally murmured.

He smiled. "Thanks for stopping in."

She caught herself wanting to say, "It was my pleasure." What a provocative admission. But a very truthful one. She had a feeling that being around Damon Trent would provide her life with more pleasure, and perhaps more pain, than she had ever before experienced. The question was, could she handle whatever the future would bring?

Seven

The three-and-a-half-hour drive to the Lake of the Ozarks from St. Louis proved uneventful. Justin had arrived at the hospital in a limousine outfitted with a place for Damon to stretch out and still leave Elise with room to be comfortable.

Both Damon and Justin appeared to take the luxury for granted, and Elise was reminded of how different their world was from the one she knew. Were their values as different? Was she the only person in the world who believed in exclusive commitment to one other person? She wondered how it was possible for a person to feel as she was already feeling toward Damon and consider being with someone else. She had no desire to be around another man, to share the intimacies she wanted to share with Damon.

Regardless of what the next three weeks would bring into her life, Elise knew that she would never feel toward anyone else what she felt for Damon. It was a frightening feeling. It gave him a certain power over her she wasn't sure she wanted to give to anyone.

She had loved Guy Brandon with a singleness of purpose that had blinded her to his shortcomings. So what had caused the sense of betrayal? Was it the love she had felt for him, or the fact that by allowing herself to be blinded to his less-than-perfect traits she was forced to acknowledge that her perception of him had been at fault? And if it had been her perception of him that had been in error, how could she hold him responsible?

"Where are we?" Damon asked Justin, effectively interrupting Elise's convoluted thoughts.

"About fifteen miles north of Jeff City," Justin replied.

Elise stared out the window. The softly rolling hills had increased the farther west they went. She had driven to Kansas City several times on I-70 but had never gone south into the center of the state.

Her first view of the state capitol made her catch her breath. Sitting on the banks of the wide Missouri River, the graceful dome proclaimed to the travelers that they had reached Jefferson City.

"How large is Jeff City?" she asked.

When Damon remained silent, Justin responded. "Around 35,000, I think."

"It seems strange in a state with large cities like Kansas City and St. Louis to have the state capitol so small."

"It's my guess the location is central to most parts of the state."

"How much farther do we have to go?"

"About fifty miles."

Within minutes they were through the city and following the well-kept highway southward, watching the rolling hills become more pronounced. Elise found herself eager to reach Damon's home, to discover more about him.

He seemed tired, as though he hadn't slept well the night before. Elise could certainly understand that. She had left his room and gone back to work feeling as though he'd started a generator deep within her that no amount of concentration on her job could turn down or off. Her body had clamored for release and she had gone home to a soaking bath and a very boring book in hopes of finding peace in sleep. Nothing had seemed to work.

She could feel the tension between them but had no idea how to combat it. She wondered if Justin was aware of the tension. If so, he was ignoring it and she wished she could.

Eventually they passed Bagnall Dam. Justin pointed it out to her and explained that it had been installed by the Union Electric Company more than fifty years ago. It was one of the few privately owned dams in the United States.

Traffic on the highway slowed down as they came into a congested area of shops and restaurants, amusement parks and racetracks. The resort flavor became noticeable and Elise wondered where Damon's home was located. Somehow she had pictured privacy and quiet, something that was certainly lacking in the area they were driving through.

Several miles later they turned onto a winding road leading into what Justin termed the Horseshoe Bend area, where the Osage River, which had been dammed to form the Lake of the Ozarks, made a sharp turn, forming a large finger of land surrounded by water. Elise soon became lost in the number of roads they turned onto, and hoped she wouldn't have to find her way back to the highway on her own. Eventually they pulled up in front of a wrought-iron gate decorated with a small sign that announced in discreet script that the road was private.

Justin got out and unlocked the gate, returned to the car and drove through, then stopped and relocked the gate. The blacktop disappeared around a corner ahead of them and when he got back into the car Justin began to follow the winding road once more.

They drove for several more miles, although perhaps it only seemed that way because with every turn Elise expected to see the house. She glanced down at Damon and realized he was asleep, his rumpled hair giving him a boyish look. When she looked up again Justin was pulling into a large circular driveway in front of a stone and glass home.

Elise caught her breath. It wasn't at all what she had expected. Somehow she had imagined a splashy, ornate, ostentatious villa. Instead, the large house before her radiated warmth and hospitality. It seemed real, and lived in, and for just a moment she fully expected to see a couple of children burst through the front door to greet them.

The door did open, revealing a short, middle-aged woman with a radiant smile. Damon stirred and pushed himself into a sitting position as Justin opened the door.

"Do you need any help?" he asked quietly.

Damon shook his head.

Justin turned around and spoke to the woman who had joined him at the door. "Now that he's here, Mattie, what do you intend to do with him?" he asked with a grin.

Mattie watched as Damon eased out of the limo and stood up. "You're looking much better than I expected," she stated in a matter-of-fact voice.

Elise stepped out beside Damon, unobtrusively sliding his hand over her bent arm.

Damon chuckled. "I don't think I want to know what you expected, Mattie." He turned his head toward Elise. "This is Elise Brandon, who will be staying for a few weeks."

Since Elise wore her uniform she knew that Mattie understood why she was there. Mattie stuck out her hand.

"Pleased to meet you, Ms. Brandon."

"Please call me Elise."

"Okay. Everyone knows me as Mattie around here. They've probably forgotten I have a last name."

Elise glanced at Justin, knowing they needed to get Damon to bed before the little strength he had was gone. He immediately picked up her signal and stepping to Damon's other side, gently guided him up the shallow steps to the front door.

"Sun feels good, doesn't it?" he commented casually.

"I'd almost forgotten how good it felt," Damon responded. "What time is it?"

"A little after two. Why?"

"Oh, I thought I might rest for a while, then spend some time lying in the sun."

Justin looked over at Elise and she nodded. "Sounds good to me. I'll probably join you. How about you, Elise?"

Elise hadn't given much thought to how she would spend her days when she wasn't caring for Damon. Before she could formulate an answer, Damon spoke up.

"You brought a swimsuit, didn't you?" he demanded.

"Yes."

"Good. Put it on. I hope it's skimpy."

The slightly wicked tone caught her off guard. What difference could it make to him what she wore?

"Actually, it's rather modest, why?"

"I've discovered the best way to get to know someone while I'm without my eyesight is to 'braille' them. I thought I'd wait until you were in a swimsuit before I asked."

"That's all right, Damon. I'll be glad to tell you what I look like."

"Somehow that just wouldn't be the same."

Justin led them down a long hallway and opened a door. The generous-sized room was mostly glass on three sides. Outside one window was a thick cluster of oak trees, so dense Elise could barely see into them. The other two sides displayed a panoramic view of the lake. The sunlight and color caught at Elise's senses. Boats with billowing sails danced upon the waves caused by speedboats hauling skiers. Sliding glass doors led from the bedroom to a rock-laid terrace, complete with lounging chairs and a table crowned with a bright-yellow umbrella.

"This is beautiful, Damon. No wonder you were anxious to come home."

He sat on the edge of the bed. "It's good to get away from the antiseptic smell of that damned hospital."

Elise smiled. He was definitely feeling better.

"Is there anything I can do?" Justin asked from the doorway.

"Why don't you show Elise where she'll be staying?" Damon suggested.

Elise obligingly followed Justin out of the room and down the hallway to another door. The room, obviously used for guests, was spacious and one wall was glass, giving another view of the lake.

"This is more like a dream than a job."

"I have a feeling you're going to earn every penny, considering the mood Damon appears to be in."

"Actually I've been waiting for it. He's been too accepting of everything. I knew that coming back to familiar surroundings would intensify his awareness of the loss of his eyesight.''

"I hope they can schedule the surgery soon.''

"Justin, the surgery isn't guaranteed to restore his sight.''

"Damon expects it to.''

"I know. That's what worries me.''

"You have to understand him. He doesn't give up. He finds alternative routes, perhaps, but he won't ever admit he can't find a solution.''

"I hope for his sake that his eyesight can be restored.''

"So do I.'' He walked over to the door. "I'm glad you came, Elise. You're good for him. I told you that.''

She smiled. "He's good for me as well, you know.''

Justin's smile broadened into a grin. "It's going to be interesting to watch what happens over the next few weeks.''

The next two weeks flew by for Elise. She spent most of her time with Damon and was amazed at how rapidly he recovered his strength. He knew his way around the place,

and with her at his side he took to exploring
the paths that weaved through the wooded area
on his property.

They spent part of their time together sharing past experiences. Damon told her about
Kathleen and how they had grown up together. Because of her congenital heart condition she had always been treated as an invalid.
Her parents were considerably older than Damon's, although they had all been good
friends, and when Kathleen's parents died
within months of each other, Damon had un-
hesitatingly married her, to keep her safe and
happy. And she had been happy. So had he.

Slowly he extracted information about
Elise's marriage.

"Are you still in love with him?" he asked
her one day while they were taking a walk.

"No. To be honest, I don't think I ever was
in love with him. I was only in love with the
man I'd invented and given Guy's looks. They
bore very little resemblance to each other."

"But you've allowed what happened to
color your relationships with other men," he
pointed out.

"Yes, I have. Because I no longer trust myself. When I am attracted to someone, I'm not

sure what's causing the attraction. Am I making up traits in my mind again, projecting and pretending that I see them?''

"Is that what you think you're doing with me?''

She stopped walking. "You're different.''

"In what way?''

"I mean, you're a patient of mine, one whom I've made friends with, but that's all.''

"Is it?'' he said with a smile. His arm suddenly darted out and locked around her waist, drawing her to him. "Do you kiss all your patients the way you do me?''

Once again Elise was made aware of the strength Damon had gained. His arms felt like muscled ribbons of iron pressing her against him and he made no effort to hide his body's response to hers as she pressed tightly against him. When his mouth came down on her lips she felt totally possessed, as though being in his arms was her ultimate destiny, and she gave herself up to the sensations he created.

"Why do you deny what you feel with me?'' he muttered, burying his head in her hair.

"It's safer that way,'' she whispered raggedly.

"But you're no coward, Elise.''

"Aren't I?"

"No! You've faced your past with courage, forcing yourself to see the truth. You've quit looking for a place to stick the labels of guilt and blame. You're willing to let go of them. Yet whenever I get too close you clutch the past as though it were a security blanket that ensures that you won't get involved with anyone else."

For someone who could not see, Damon had an amazing grasp of what she had been experiencing. His insight startled her until she realized how much of his business success had been built on his ability to read people.

"Every time I come close to you, I can feel the wall rise up between us."

Elise glanced down at the way their bodies were molded together. "I don't see how a wall could possibly be inserted between us now."

He shook her slightly. "Oh, it's there. I hear it in your flippant tone of voice, I feel it in the stiffening of your body and the rapid beat of your heart. Your flight sensors are working overtime."

Elise resented his being able to read her so well. She pushed against his chest and he allowed his arms to drop. "We need to go back to the house."

"Of course, Nurse Brandon. Wrap yourself up in your professional cloak whenever I dare to get too close to you."

"What do you want from me, Damon!" she demanded.

"I want the same type of honesty that you're capable of giving to yourself. Admit that you're attracted to me. Admit that we share something very rare in the way of relationships. That we managed to skip a whole series of steps in getting to know each other because of the experiences we shared while I was in the hospital. And admit that you're afraid of getting hurt again!"

"All right! I'm terrified of getting hurt again!" she yelled, then stopped in amazement when she heard the loss of control in her voice. She, the lady who was always so controlled in her speech and manner, was screaming like a fishwife!

Damon laughed, a pleased, delighted sound. "Fantastic. And that didn't hurt a bit, did it?"

She stared at him in horror. What sort of control did this man have over her, anyway? Elise never raised her voice, no matter what the provocation. And yet with Damon she seemed to lose all control.

As much as she wanted to walk away, she couldn't leave him alone. Without saying a word, she took his arm and began to walk along the pathway.

"Are we not speaking now?" he asked whimsically.

Elise could say nothing. She knew if she opened her mouth to try to explain the conflicting emotions within her, she would burst into tears, another first for her.

Damon was very dangerous to her peace of mind.

Elise lay in bed that night watching the moon cross the sky. Damon had been in high spirits all day, partly due to a phone conversation with Justin over a business matter that obviously had worked out satisfactorily. But she felt certain he was also pleased with her outburst earlier in the day.

He had asked her to read some business journals to him that Justin had forwarded, and had excused her to go to bed when she admitted after an hour or two that she was tired.

Unfortunately, she'd been unable to sleep.

Later, she realized that had she been asleep, she wouldn't have heard the thud that brought her out of bed and on her feet. Since she slept with her door open at night in case Damon needed her, she was through the door and into his room within seconds.

From the light of the moon she could see that he was not in bed. She heard a muttered cursing coming from the bathroom.

"Damon?"

The door opened and she saw his darker shadow within.

"Are you all right?"

"I'm just great! I hit my head on the cabinet and knocked the glass off the counter when I tried to get a drink. Couldn't be better!"

She heard the pain and frustration in his voice and wished there were some way she could take it away. "Could I get you a drink?"

"You're damned right you could! Scotch on the rocks...make it a double!"

She turned away from him and felt her way back to the living room, flipping on a small lamp near the bar. Finding the Scotch, she poured a healthy amount of liquid over several ice cubes and returned to the bedroom.

Damon sat on the side of the bed, his head in his hands. Since arriving at the lake he had dispensed with pajamas. He sat there in his briefs, his tanned body gleaming in the moonlight. She knelt down beside him. "Here's your drink."

"What? No lectures about how bad the liquor is for my health? No sneers about my helplessness? But of course, you're my very own Florence Nightingale, here to do my bidding, whatever coarse things I might suggest."

"Damon, stop it! What's wrong?"

He raised his head, staring in her direction, pain and agony written across his face. "What's wrong? I'm blind, that's what's wrong. I'm thirty-nine years old, head of a business I built by myself, with more money than I could ever hope to spend in this lifetime, owner of a half-dozen homes and as many automobiles, and I'm reduced to stumbling around in the dark like a child, unable to even go to the bathroom by myself!"

He took a large swallow of his drink, stroking his thumb against the chilled exterior of the glass.

"You seemed so happy earlier this evening."

"Oh, I was. Everything's going as planned. My business is operating smoothly without me, I've got a gorgeous nurse staying with me who jumps three feet every time I touch her, and I'm slowly losing my mind in the perennial darkness I've inhabited for the past three months. What more could I ask for in life?"

"Patience, perhaps?" she asked softly.

He had raised his glass halfway to his mouth and paused at her words. "Is that all you think it takes?" he asked. "Will patience give me back my eyesight and teach you to love me?"

Her breath caught in her throat. Never had she heard that tone of voice from him before, almost a tone of entreaty. "Is that what you want, Damon?"

He lifted his drink and finished it, setting it down on the table by the bed. "I don't know anymore. Maybe you're right. Once I get my sight back and my life returns to normal, I'll probably forget all about you. I've just used you as a fantasy figure in my life these past few months to overcome the boredom."

Elise took one of his hands and rested it on her cheek. "Which one of us are you trying to convince now?"

"Me, of course. You've been convinced all the time that I couldn't possibly be interested in you, the person."

Slowly Elise rose to her feet. "Oh, Damon. Why do we make something hard out of something so simple?" She sat down on the bed beside him. "Of course I love you. I've known that for some time. But you're right. Your life isn't normal right now and I think it would be better to wait until your surgery is over before we make any decisions."

"Just in case, huh? You wouldn't want to be stuck with a blind man for the rest of your life."

"Oh, I don't know. I could certainly count on your not chasing other women then."

"Like Guy."

"I didn't say that."

"You didn't have to. I always feel that he's here in the room with us. Can you imagine what it would be like in bed together—you, me and Guy?"

He sounded so disgusted that Elise bubbled over in laughter. It really sounded so ridiculous, and of course he was right. Unconsciously she still compared his behavior to Guy's.

"You weren't supposed to laugh," he said plaintively. "I was doing my best to insult you, make you mad, make you angry enough to yell at me again."

She stared at him in surprise. "But why?"

"Because I want to wake you up from the dream state you're living in. I want you to be aware of the here and now, and get out of the past. Do you have any idea what you're missing?"

"Would you like to show me?"

She heard the sudden inhalation of his breath. Her provocative statement had caught him off guard. He paused in his vehement speech. Now it was her turn.

"The here and now has me sitting next to you on your bed in the middle of the night with you wearing nothing but very skimpy briefs and me in my nightgown. What would you like to do with the here and the now, Damon?"

Uncertainly he reached out to her, accidentally brushing her breast. He jerked his fingers as though they were burned and moved his hand up to her jaw. His fingers traced the slight smile on her face and his own face relaxed.

"I could have set up the seduction scene a little better than this, don't you think?"

"Well, the lecture detracts from the mood somewhat."

His hand slipped behind her neck and he leaned closer, his lips brushing hers. "If you're teasing me, Elise, don't carry it any further. I'm a very hungry man and you are the juiciest morsel I've ever wanted in my life."

Elise slid both her arms around his waist. She could feel the heavy thudding of his chest and recognized that the game, if it had ever been that, had suddenly turned into a very serious one.

When had she decided to give their relationship a chance? During the sleepless hours she'd just spent thinking of all they had discussed? Had she known what she intended when she came into his room tonight?

Her hands smoothed across his chest and she felt him catch his breath. This was no longer a game, and all the rules that Elise Brandon had used to govern her life until now were discarded.

Whatever was to happen between them would happen. She could no longer fight both of them. She didn't even want to fight, not any longer. Not with the scent of his after-shave filling her senses, the smooth touch of his chest beckoning her fingertips and the firm feel of his lips hovering over hers.

With a soft sigh, she closed the distance between them.

Eight

Eight

Moonlight filtered through the gauzy curtains, giving a soft glow to the room. A certain sense of rightness pervaded Elise's senses when she felt herself drawn down into Damon's arms as he lowered them onto the bed.

How many months had she pictured herself with him, loving him, opening herself up to his love? His gentle, unhurried touch caught at her attention. He was not going to rush her. But then he had never rushed her, never in the weeks and months she had known him. He had given her the space to become familiar with him, to learn more and more about who he was. He had given her the time to fall in love with him.

She found herself anticipating his lovemaking, knowing that being in his arms was the most important thing in her life at the moment.

"You feel so good here with me, Elise," he murmured. "I've needed you so much, but I was afraid."

"You're not afraid of anything, Damon."

"Oh, yes. My biggest fear has been that some careless remark might frighten you away from me before I had the chance to come closer."

His mouth settled contentedly on hers and began a sensuous exploration; his tongue probed until she allowed him entrance. He shifted and his knee gently nudged her legs apart. When she relaxed he slid his leg intimately between hers, drawing her close to his body, so that the warmth of his thigh sent a charge of electricity throughout her body.

Her gown became a hindrance, and he brushed the straps down off her shoulders. She pulled her arms out, then nestled them around his shoulders while his hands pushed the offending article of clothing down her body. It lay in a soft circle around her hips and he sighed with contentment when his mouth found the taut, upward thrust of her breast. She gave a convulsive quiver as he pulled the tip into his mouth, playfully wrapping his tongue around it, then claiming it with a serious intent.

Elise discovered she was holding her breath and she forced herself to exhale. She was quivering from the intensity of her feelings, unable to concentrate, until she finally gave up trying to think and instead relaxed, resigned to feeling the new sensations that only Damon was able to evoke deep within her.

She loved him and she wanted to express that love. She wanted him to feel the same sensations he was eliciting within her.

Damon felt Elise quiver under his inquisitive hands. Her skin felt so smooth and soft and he reveled in his sudden freedom to explore her mysteries. He felt swallowed up in the fresh floral scent that he always associated with her.

Never had he felt his lack of sight so keenly as at this moment when he wanted so desperately to gaze into her eyes, to see her expression, to know beyond a shadow of a doubt that she wanted him as much as he wanted her—that she needed him and loved him with the same intensity he was feeling. Instead, he could go only by her responses. He felt so vulnerable at a moment in time when he needed to be sure, not only of what was happening but also of her willingness to share love—in its most physical sense—with him.

"Oh, Damon," he heard her say softly. Then he felt her touch him intimately, her hand gently stroking his unyielding flesh. His heart bounded and he raised his head from her breast. She moved restlessly, her fingers quivering against him and he recognized her action for what it was. She wanted him, too. She was encouraging him to take her to the outer limits of physical sensation.

Damon needed no further urging. He slipped the gown from her hips, then lowered himself so that he lay between her legs, her soft warmth cradling his manhood while it pulsed its need for possession. With a groan, Damon thrust deep inside her, glorying in her ability to accept him without discomfort, her warmth enveloping him, pulling him ever closer to her innermost being.

Her arms clasped his neck and his mouth
fastened on hers with fierce possession. His
tongue kept rhythm with his body, each thrust
expressing his joy of her, each thrust a statement of ecstasy, of potential fulfillment, of
love long postponed.

Elise couldn't understand what was happening to her. She couldn't get enough of him.
Her body had ignited, bursting like an incen-
diary bomb into flames that seemed to con-
sume them both. Forgotten were her fears of
the future, or thoughts of the past. Damon had
her total attention and concentration. She was
aware of nothing else but him.

His arms tightened convulsively around her
and he made one final lunge that seemed to
destroy the gravity that held them to the
planet. Together they soared through the uni-
verse, scattering stars, watching others burst,
while still wrapped in each other's arms.

Damon's head rested heavily on the pillow
beside her, his body limply splayed across her.
For the first time since she'd heard him earlier
in the night, Elise thought of his injuries.

During the weeks they had been at the lake
she tried to reassure herself that his strength
had steadily returned. His lungs seemed to be

all right, she thought with a smile. She felt the slow, deep breathing that spoke of restful sleep. Gingerly she shifted so that she could feel the scar of his surgery. After almost three months he had healed nicely, but she was appalled to recognize that never during their earlier activity had she given his physical condition a thought.

His breathing continued to be slow and steady and his heart quietly thudded against her. He certainly didn't make love like an invalid, she decided with a slight smile, remembering his stamina.

Elise drifted off to sleep, still held closely in Damon's arms.

When she awoke she had no doubt where she was. Damon still held her to him in a close embrace and he was contentedly nibbling on her neck.

The room had begun to lighten, but the sun hadn't as yet appeared. "You must be hungry," she whispered.

"Absolutely starved," he admitted, while he continued to blaze a trail down her throat with his mouth.

"Would you like me to make you some breakfast?" she asked breathlessly. His hand had slid unobtrusively down her abdomen and rested at the apex of her thighs. His fingers shifted restlessly, with no apparent pattern until they suddenly found the place for which they were searching. She arched unconsciously into his hand.

"I've already found breakfast, thank you," he replied with a chuckle. Leaning over her, he unerringly found her mouth with his, and leisurely explored her lips, running his tongue over the slightly irregular ridge of her lower teeth. "I can't seem to get enough of you," he finally admitted, pulling back from her for a moment.

"Don't overdo, love. You haven't been out of the hospital that long, remember," she whispered, hating to be the one to remind them of possible limitations to expressing their love.

"I'd forgotten," he admitted. Slowly he lowered himself to the bed once more while his other arm, securely tucked underneath Elise, pulled her unprotestingly on top of him. "So, Nurse Brandon, what do you suggest? Would it help if I were to just lie here?" he offered with a slight smile.

The early daylight gave her a clear picture of the man lying immediately beneath her loving gaze. His wide forehead looked smooth and untroubled, the thin white line across his brows the only evidence of the tremendous blow he'd received. His high cheekbones were prominent but the flesh below them had begun to fill in the gaunt planes and angles.

Damon's eyes shone like silver glass, his long, thick lashes forming a lush frame around them. They gazed at her with such a clear expression of love that it was hard for her to believe there was no sight within them.

He shifted, causing her attention to refocus to other parts of his anatomy that were also alive and well, and seeking entrance. Elise had only to shift slightly to accommodate him, and suddenly they were locked together once again, experiencing the same indescribable sensations of the night before.

Elise tried to concentrate on not hurting him in any way but it was so hard to think when she was feeling such a wild sense of excitement. Never before had she considered the mutual possession that occurs during lovemaking, the pleasurable give-and-take of sharing the intimacy of love. She forced herself to set an easy rhythm, where she did most of the moving and he—from the obvious enjoyment on his face—

appeared willing to relax and enjoy her temporary domination.

Where the night before had been a sudden explosion, almost cataclysmic in its intensity, the morning had brought a certain peace and mutual certainty that what they shared was special, and therefore never-ending, so that the need to rush was gone. A need to savor and to enjoy enveloped them, and they clung to each other in a profound awareness of what they had discovered.

Somewhere along the way Elise lost the slow rhythm, however, and became caught up in the urgency of sensation. Damon's hands settled around her hips and continued to guide her. Their breaths were coming in shortened pants and the coiled spring deep inside her seemed to be turning ever tighter until suddenly it snapped and she let out a cry.

"That's the way, love, let it go," he whispered in a husky voice, pulling her down to him in a tight embrace. He followed her quickly over the edge of control and into total sensation and pleasure, and they lay there, wrapped in each other's arms, until Elise was once again aware of where she was, who she was . . . and that Damon did not need her extra weight on his chest.

She quickly slid to his side but could not move any farther. He held her clutched to him much like a young child with its cuddly doll. "Don't leave," he admonished.

Elise tried to laugh but was still having trouble with her breathing. "I can barely move, much less leave," she managed to gasp.

Damon's sigh of satisfaction expanded his chest for an instant, then was gone. "Good. I don't want you to leave. Not ever."

Not ever? Elise thought about that for a moment. In that moment she visualized what it would mean to be able to stay with Damon, to travel with him, be a part of his life, perhaps even have his children. What would it mean to commit herself totally to this man? Did he even want a commitment from her? They had never discussed a future before. Now she was afraid to. She felt like a child in a giant toy store with all the glittering choices in front of her. All she needed to do was to choose. But she was afraid. What if she made another mistake?

Once again Elise fell asleep in Damon's arms. When she awoke she was alone. She heard the shower running in Damon's bathroom and glanced at her watch. It was almost ten o'clock.

How could she have slept so long? She wondered if Mattie had looked for her. If so, she would have discovered she wasn't in her bedroom. Elise could feel the sudden heat climb through her body at the thought. As attractive as Damon was, she was certain that he had brought many women down to the lake to visit. But her role down here had not been as a playmate, but rather as his nurse.

Grabbing her gown from the floor, she hastily slid it on and went back to her room. Nothing had been disturbed. She went on into the bathroom and took a shower, hoping to gather her scattered thoughts. What had happened last night had changed their relationship irrevocably.

Was she ready to handle the change? Elise wasn't at all sure.

By the time she was dressed and courageous enough to face the world, Elise found Damon on the terrace attacking a heavily laden plate of breakfast. He glanced up at her step and gave her a broad, gleaming grin. "Good morning. Did you sleep well?"

Elise sat down opposite him and concentrated on pouring herself a cup of coffee. "I slept quite well," she offered in a repressed tone, "as you very well know."

His smile wavered slightly as he put his fork down on his plate and stared in her direction. "What's wrong?" he asked in a flat tone.

"I'm just not sure of the proper etiquette in a situation like this."

"Like what?" A frown appeared on his face.

"There's no telling what Mattie must be thinking about me now."

"Do you care?"

"Yes. Well, not really. I mean—"

"You mean that *you* aren't sure what to think about you, isn't that what's bothering you?"

She was quiet while she thought about his question. Taking a sip of her coffee, she eventually nodded. "Yes. I can't imagine what I was thinking of last night."

"Could it be possible you were allowing yourself the opportunity to feel, to relate, to enjoy, without the necessity of thinking every damned minute?"

She examined the harsh planes in his face as he stared at her, his gaze piercing her as though she were a butterfly pinned to a board and his gaze the pin.

How could she possibly answer him? —

He sighed. Carefully feeling for his coffee mug, he raised it to his lips and drank. Elise heard the sliding door open and glanced around. Mattie stuck her head out.

"What would you like for breakfast, Elise?" she said with a friendly grin. Mattie had greeted her in a similar fashion every morning since she'd arrived. Why had Elise expected anything different?

"Maybe some toast and some fruit," she acknowledged with a smile.

Mattie nodded and disappeared inside the house once again.

"I'm really very mixed up this morning," Elise finally admitted in the silence.

"So I've noticed," Damon drawled.

"I'm not used to going to bed with my patients, Damon!"

He laughed at her vehemence. "I'm very pleased to hear that, Elise. I'm much more reassured about the entire situation now that you've clarified it for me."

His teasing had always been one of his most endearing qualities to her—until now. At the moment she would have gladly shoved him in the lake, had he been closer to the edge.

She glared at him, aware that even that small bit of defiance was wasted on him. Elise was grateful when Mattie showed up with her breakfast, and even more grateful when she discovered that Mattie was not alone.

"Good morning, you two," Justin greeted them, striding to the table.

"Justin! It's good to see you," Elise admitted with a great deal of honesty.

Damon heard the relief in her voice. She was temporarily off the hook and she knew it. Damn Justin and his impeccable sense of timing. "What are you doing here?" he asked less than graciously.

Justin laughed. "Your mood hasn't seemed to change much in the past two weeks. It's a wonder Elise has been able to tolerate you." He glanced at her and noticed her heightened color. Had he interrupted something? "Has he been this grouchy for the past two weeks?" he asked in a sympathetic tone.

Feeling suddenly lighthearted, Elise gave Damon a mischievous glance and winked at

Justin. "Not really. He can be an absolute lamb as long as things go exactly the way he wants. Sometime during his past Mr. Trent must have gotten the idea that everything has to go his way."

Damon scowled, recognizing the teasing relief in her voice and acknowledging to himself that she was much more relaxed with Justin than she was around him. Damn his eyes and his inability to watch her expression!

"I'm afraid I've contributed to his misconception, Elise," Justin admitted in a pseudo-sad voice. "If I don't strive to keep him happy, he's always threatening to fire me. Then where would I be? My wife and family would starve, not to mention my widowed mother, my—"

"Oh, for God's sake!" Damon set his coffee mug down with a thud. "You aren't even married, Justin, and unless your dad has died since I last talked with you, your parents are presently rollicking on the shores of Maui, soaking up some sun."

Justin's grin grew even wider. "Of course, being around Damon does ensure that I keep an honest tongue about me."

"Hah!"

"Otherwise, he's quick to point out my shortcomings."

"Of which you have many."

"See what I mean?"

Elise was laughing at the banter between the two men, who obviously held each other in high regard. The tension slipped away from the moment and for the next several hours the three of them enjoyed the sun.

Justin took them out on a cabin cruiser stored in a boat dock down by the shore. Elise finally got up enough nerve to wear the new bikini she had bought at one of the boutiques along the strip near the dam. There wasn't much to it, which enabled her to deepen her tan.

She was pleased with how well she looked, she thought while gathering her things together in the bedroom. The sun had lightened her hair in streaks, and her skin was a deep-bronzed color. Her face glowed with vitality and the lively sparkle in her eyes loudly proclaimed her feelings for Damon.

Thank God he couldn't see her. Otherwise there would be no eluding him in his relentless search for her innermost feelings.

After carefully covering her body with sun-tan lotion Elise stretched out in the sunshine, enjoying the gently rolling waves and cool breeze. Both Justin and Damon wore rather brief swimsuits that fit them very well. Both men were tall and well built, and Elise really couldn't understand how she could be so relaxed and at ease with Justin, completely unmoved by his blond good looks, and be so tense and on edge around Damon. Damon had always had that effect on her, even during his early days in the hospital.

She enjoyed watching the two men talking. Justin was in the captain's seat, slouched down with one foot on the rung, the other stretched out in front of him. Damon stood nearby, facing into the gentle breeze, listening to Justin.

Later in the afternoon Elise glanced up in time to see Justin take a picture of her.

"What are you doing?" she demanded.

"What does it look like I'm doing?"

"I mean, why did you take a picture of me?"

"Just practicing my skills. Can't let them get rusty." The truth would probably have made her uncomfortable. Damon had asked him to take pictures of her and to have them blown up for him. He was still talking as though it were only a matter of time before he'd be able to enjoy looking at them.

Justin couldn't get over the change in Elise in two short weeks. She had blossomed. It wasn't just the tan and the new, freer hair-style. There was a lilt in her voice, a spring to her step and a glow in her face that hadn't been there before. Whatever had been going on be-tween her and Damon, and it was obvious from the tension that something was happen-ing, it had been good for both of them.

However, he didn't want to see either one of them hurt. The situation was very uncertain and he could only hope that things would work out for them.

It was only when they brought the boat in to the dock late that afternoon that Justin began to worry about the delicate status of the rela-tionship forming between Damon and Elise.

Cynthia Rydell stood waiting on the dock in a bright sunsuit, waving gaily.

"Damon? Did you invite Cynthia to the lake?" he asked quietly.

Damon's head snapped around and he stared in Justin's direction. "You know better than that!"

"Well, she's on the dock waiting for us. Thought you'd want a warning of sorts."

The muttered imprecations delivered just below his breath were enough to turn the air blue around Damon, and Justin had all he could do not to laugh. He had had a hunch Cynthia would not be put off for long, but he didn't feel any better for being correct. From all indications, the situation between Damon and Elise was very fragile at the moment.

He hoped Cynthia wasn't going to throw a monkey wrench in the works!

Nine

Elise had enjoyed her afternoon out on the lake. Part of her enjoyment had to do with Justin's presence. While Damon had been relaxed and entertained by Justin's tales of high finance and big city machinations, she had been given the opportunity to sit back quietly and watch Damon to her heart's content.

He bore little resemblance to the man she'd first seen battling for his life in the hospital. Now he was brown and fit, eager to return to the life he thrived on. She knew they had things to discuss, but she wasn't ready to face the consequences of what she had allowed to happen the night before.

Elise wished she could pretend it had been an accident, not to be repeated. She knew better. What they had shared was not some one-night stand to be ignored the next day. However, thanks to Justin's arrival, she had a little more time to decide what to say to Damon.

The boat began to slow and turn toward shore and Elise sat up. She saw a woman standing on the dock they were approaching, a warm smile accompanying her waving hand. Elise felt her heart slide heavily into her stomach and lodge there, refusing to resume its normal position. Cynthia Rydell had arrived.

Glancing around, she noticed that Justin and Damon were talking, but she couldn't hear what they were saying. Damon's face registered no expression at all. Never had she seen it so blank and she wondered what that portended. She caught Justin's gaze for a moment and he smiled reassuringly at her.

What did Justin know about her and Damon? Had he guessed? Did it show to everyone who saw her that she was in love with him? She felt herself stiffen at the thought. Cynthia Rydell was the very last person Elise would want to recognize the depths of her feelings for Damon.

Many years ago Elise had enjoyed participating in her high school drama club. Frantically she called upon all her thespian skills to get her through the evening as Damon Trent's nurse. Would she be able to appear friendly but professional? A great deal would depend on how Damon reacted to Cynthia's presence.

He hadn't wanted her to see him in the hospital, but that wasn't unusual. He had been at a definite disadvantage back then, and he'd resented the sympathy of those around him. Now that he was well, except for his eyes, he might be eager for Cynthia to join him. If that were the case, it made all that had happened between them the night before a mockery, but what did Elise know or understand about the male animal and his instincts?

Whatever happened, Elise did not intend to let anyone know how painfully she anticipated the coming evening.

The moment that Cynthia spied Elise, her smile disappeared from her face and her body stiffened. Elise carefully stood up, keeping her balance as the slowing boat rocked over the waves coming in to shore. She knew that Damon was waiting for her to guide him back to the house.

They had worked out a comfortable way for him to get around the area without having to use a walking stick. He refused to consider one, insisting that for the short time he would be without his sight, he didn't need a cane. Elise prayed that he was right. In the house he knew his way around. Fortunately there was only the one level for him to navigate. Outside was a different matter—and that was where Elise came in.

She reached Damon's side at the same time Justin guided them into the slip. Instead of taking her arm, as was his custom, he wrapped his arm securely around her waist and leaned down and kissed her, his kiss landing near her ear.

Elise glanced up at him in surprise, then quickly looked back at the young woman standing on the dock watching them, her hands on her hips. "What are you doing?" she whispered to Damon as she tried to look relaxed and unconcerned. "Cynthia Rydell is here."

Contentedly nuzzling her ear, Damon murmured, "So what?"

Justin cut the engine and secured the boat. He didn't help matters by saying, "Okay, you two, we're here," thereby calling unnecessary attention to them.

With a wide smile, Damon replied, "Glad to hear it. I'm about ready for a nap." He glanced down at her, his eyes gleaming wickedly. "How about you?"

Cynthia could not help but overhear the conversation, as she was standing only a few feet away. "You look completely recovered, darling. The air must agree with you," she said to Damon in a soft drawl.

Elise felt invisible.

Damon ignored Cynthia's remark. With admirable nonchalance he placed Elise's arm around his waist, then nudged her to lead them off the boat. Since the area was too narrow for two abreast, he slid his hands to her waist and followed her off the boat. As soon as he was on the dock, however, his arm wrapped around Elise's waist once more.

With a certain amount of detached interest, Elise watched the various emotions rush across Cynthia's face. There was no way Elise was going to get free of Damon, he was making sure of that. She decided not to try.

"Why, Cynthia," he finally responded in a smooth tone, "what a surprise. We weren't expecting you."

Cynthia's face was flushed and her lips had narrowed to a thin, unbecoming line. "That's obvious. Aren't you even going to introduce us?" She looked Elise up and down as though certain Damon had fished her out of some disreputable hole.

"Oh, I thought you'd already met." He glanced around. "Justin? Are you there?"

Justin stepped over to Damon's other side and began to guide them toward the steps.

"Didn't Cynthia meet Elise at the hospital?" Damon inquired.

Cynthia fell into step behind them. "The hospital! You mean you've known her that long?"

Once again they needed to walk single file. Elise took the lead and the others followed. No one answered Cynthia's remark until they were inside the comfortably large living area of Damon's home. Elise smiled at Cynthia. "I'm not surprised you don't remember me. You were very upset the night you were in to see him." She glanced at the other two men who stood waiting for her to make the explanations. "I was the nurse in charge of Damon in the intensive care unit.''

Cynthia's face turned white, then flushed an unbecoming red. She stared at the woman in front of her, her long legs tanned a deep bronze, her small waist emphasizing the gentle curve of her hips, her gauzy cover-up failing to hide the curves of her breasts barely covered by the bikini she wore.

"You mean you're Damon's nurse?" she demanded.

Damon grinned. He ran his finger along Elise's arm, causing a row of chills to run up her arm. "Among other things," he murmured, loud enough to be heard by everyone in the room.

What was he trying to do? Elise wondered with dismay. He'd been perfectly correct in front of Justin the entire day. Now he was making it clear to everyone that there was more between them than a nurse-patient relationship. Damn him, anyway!

"Would anyone care for a drink?" Justin asked with a grin. He was obviously enjoying all of this, Elise decided. Men! Would she ever be able to understand them?

"Not for me," Damon replied. "I need to get a shower." He clasped Elise's hand. "We'll see you two later," he added, and started down the long hallway with Elise following him.

Justin wished he had his camera with him. The expression on Cynthia's face was indescribable. It was too bad that Damon had to miss it.

"Would you kindly explain to me what the hell is going on?" Cynthia demanded.

Justin took a sip of his drink and sighed in appreciation. "Sure you don't want a drink, Cynthia?"

"Yes, as a matter of fact I do. I'd like a martini. A very dry martini," she added in a hard tone.

"One martini coming up."

"How long has she been here?"

"Who, Elise? Oh, ever since Damon left the hospital."

"And just when was that? I noticed that no one bothered to let me know."

"A little more than two weeks ago."

"He looks through me as though I don't even exist," she muttered, taking the proffered drink from Justin.

"That isn't intentional, Cynthia," he responded in a gentle voice. "Damon is blind."

"What? But he can't be! He doesn't have any trouble getting around."

"Most of that is because of Elise. When they first got here she helped him count the number of steps to cross each room and to go down the hallway. Mattie was cautioned not to rearrange the furniture. And Elise is always with him whenever he goes outside."

Cynthia sank into the plushness of the long sofa that faced the massive stone fireplace. "Blind! How horrible. How can he endure it!" she said with a shudder. Glancing at the drink in her hand with surprise at its presence she took a large swallow in an obvious effort to gain control of herself.

Justin studied the woman in front of him. The red strapless sunsuit she wore flattered her figure, showing off her petite form. Her black curls were pulled up in back, causing a cascade of waves to fall provocatively around her shoulders. She was a very good-looking woman. He knew that Damon had enjoyed her company. But she wasn't Elise.

If Justin had had any doubts about Damon's feelings before today, those doubts were

now laid to rest. Justin had never seen Damon
so openly affectionate with another woman as
he was with Elise. His teasing was something
new, and the hard lines had disappeared in his
face. He was happy. Justin shook his head in
disbelief. Damon treated his blindness as a
temporary, even minor, condition. He'd found
contentment in Elise's presence.

He had taken some snapshots of Elise that
day that showed her love for Damon. Her face
was so expressive and Justin had enjoyed
watching her watch Damon. He was pleased
for both of them, and fully intended to see that
Cynthia did not cause trouble.

"So what brought you to the lake, Cynthia?"

"I thought that was obvious, Justin. I came
to see Damon."

"Don't you think it would have been wiser
to wait for an invitation?" he asked smoothly.

Cynthia glared at him before taking another swallow of her drink. "Damon and I are
much further along in our relationship than
that, Justin, and you know it. But I can understand why he didn't ask me down here."

*Good for you, Cynthia. Then you under-
stand you are no longer a part of Damon's life.*

"Yes. He didn't want me to know about his blindness." She sat forward and stared up at Justin. "How bad is it? Can they do anything for him?"

Justin stared at the woman in amazement. How was she able to totally ignore Elise's presence?

"They intend to do surgery in a few weeks. But no one will guarantee the success of it."

"Poor Damon. Trying to fight his battles all alone."

Justin sat down in a large, overstuffed chair across from her. "He hasn't been exactly alone, Cynthia," he pointed out dryly.

Cynthia shrugged. "But that's Damon. He's a normal, healthy male and he's not going to sleep alone if he can help it. Now that I'm here, I'm sure all of that will change."

A slight shiver went down Justin's backbone. Such implacable determination chilled him. Had Damon ever seen that part of her, or had he been too caught up in the little-girl act she portrayed? She reminded him of an antiballistic missile locked in on her target. Nothing was going to distract her from her goal, and Damon was obviously what she was after.

Damon was handicapped by his lack of sight at the moment, and Justin found himself worrying about his friend. But Damon was a grown man and could look after himself. Justin raised his glass in a mock toast to Cynthia. "How long do you intend to stay?"

She was studying her drink when he spoke and she raised her lashes and peered through them. Giving him a secret smile she answered, "As long as it takes, Justin."

Damon reached his bedroom and swept Elise through the doorway. Then he closed the door and locked it. "Ah, alone at last. I didn't think I'd ever get you all to myself again," he said. He pulled Elise into his arms and began to kiss her with a slow, mind-drugging expertise that caused her knees to buckle.

"Damon," she protested when she could find her breath.

"Yes, love," he murmured, his hands finding and loosening the ties to her bikini top. It dropped carelessly to the floor and he felt the weight of her breasts in his palms. He had her leaning against the door and he lowered his head, eager to taste the richness that was Elise.

"We need to talk," she managed to say in a breathless voice. Her eyes were closed and her head was thrown back, her body full of myriad sensations.

She felt more than heard his chuckle. Her hands rested on his shoulders in order to keep her balance and she felt the slight vibration of his amusement.

"Later, my love. We'll no doubt find many hours left in which we can talk." He turned and strode toward the bathroom with sure steps, once again pulling her behind him. "But first, you need to scrub my back. I'll even scrub yours in return."

He stepped out of his bathing suit with supreme nonchalance, his body showing its reaction to hers. Then he turned and, catching his thumbs just under the sides of her bikini bottoms, slid them down her long, curving legs.

Damon felt on fire with need and love for Elise. He could feel her body quivering at his touch and he laid his face against her abdomen. She smelled so good and he loved her so much. He could feel her warmth radiating through him and he felt a fierce need to possess her.

Standing up, he reached into the shower and turned it on, adjusting the temperature, then he turned around and picked her up.

Pulling her thighs around his waist, he stepped into the shower.

"Damon, you'll hurt yourself," she managed to say.

He placed her hips on the slight ledge that circled the shower, just enough to take her weight off him, but he kept her where she was, open and ready for him. With one smooth motion, he entered her, smiling at the moist readiness that suddenly surrounded him. Then his mouth found hers and his tongue began the same rhythm, stroking, plunging, withdrawing, plunging once again.

"Oh . . . Damon . . . we shouldn't be . . . you could hurt yourself . . . oooooh . . . Damon. . . ."

Elise lost track of time and where they were, the warm water splashing over them causing a surrealistic state for her. When Damon's arms tightened convulsively around her she moaned in response, for the fireworks were shooting off again deep inside her, and her hands loosened their hold around his neck. She felt as though she were melting down his body.

Damon lowered her legs until she was standing upright, but he kept his arms around her. She felt limp in his arms. "Are you okay?" he managed to ask when he could get his breath.

She could only nod but since her head was resting against his chest, he understood. Damon reached for the soap and began to explore her body with soft, loving strokes. He loved the feel of her body. Her skin felt like satin. Justin had told him that she had turned a dark golden brown in the sun. He wished he could see her. He ran his hands through her hair. Unbound as it was, it fell several inches below her shoulders. It felt thick and lustrous to him.

Turning her to the wall he carefully soaped her back, feeling the slight indentation of her spine under his hands. Her waist was so small he could span it with his hands and he was delighted to discover dimplelike indentations where her hips curved outward and formed cheeks.

Elise drew a ragged breath. "It's my turn." She turned around and took the soap from him. She couldn't take her eyes off his mouth, the firm upper lip, the lower one fuller, the curve causing an inner response from her. She caught his lower lip between her teeth and gently pulled on it all the while she lathered his chest, rubbing her hands from his shoulders to his thighs.

He groaned and she let go. "Did I hurt you?" she whispered. He shook his head. Her hands swept downward once again and her fingers brushed against his manhood. He was rigid and she blinked. Hastily she moved behind him and began to rub his back vigorously. When she was through she laid the soap back in its dish. "There," she tried to say in a matter-of-fact voice, but there was a catch in her tone. "You're all clean."

"Thank you," he murmured, rinsing himself. The soap he had placed on her had disappeared while she had lathered him, and Elise stepped out of the shower. As soon as Damon turned off the water, she handed him a towel. He quickly used it, standing between her and the door. After she had dried off, including towel-drying her hair, she attempted to step around him.

His arm came up, stopping her. Still without speaking he guided her back into the bedroom, where the late-afternoon sun made patterns through the vertical blinds. He led her across to the bed and pulled her down with him.

"Don't leave just yet. Stay with me a little while longer." He began to kiss her, soft, affectionate kisses—on her eyes, her nose, along her cheek, the sides of her mouth.

"I need to get my clothes."

"I had Mattie move your things in here today. They're hanging in the closet."

"Damon! You had no right to do that without asking me."

"I know." He continued to kiss her, and Elise discovered how difficult it was to concentrate while lying nude next to Damon who was also nude. His kisses weren't helping her powers of concentration, either.

"What about Cynthia?"

"What about her?" He was now tracing a path down her collarbone and over to her left breast.

"What will she think?"

"Who cares?"

"But if you're going to marry her..."

He paused in his explorations and raised his head. "Where in the world did you get that idea?"

"She introduced herself at the hospital as your fiancée."

"I have no control over how the woman introduces herself. But she knows very well I never have had any intention of marrying her."

A slight shiver ran down Elise's spine at the coldness in his tone. Damon felt the quiver. "Elise. I have never made promises to anyone I didn't intend to keep. I have several that I want to make to you, but I'm not going to make them until after my surgery. I have no intention of asking you to spend your life with a blind man."

Her heart leaped at his comments and she stared at him.

"But you had better be prepared to answer some heavy questions once I know I can see again, because I don't want to lose you from my life. Do you understand me?"

"I think so."

"Good." He nodded his head. "Now. Where was I?" Once again he lowered his head to her breast, his tongue teasing her.

"Oh, Damon, I'm not sure about any of this."

"That's all right. I'm sure enough for both of us." He leaned forward and found her

mouth with his and began an assault that left
her totally defenseless against him.

By the time he had eased his long length over
hers she had forgotten everything but him once
more. He had a rather unnerving habit of doing that to her. It was beginning to feel natural
and very familiar to have him close to her like
that.

She shifted slightly, raising her hips to meet
his, and he chuckled. He knew of her resistance to responding to a commitment where he
was concerned. Damon wasn't sure how much
of it had to do with his lack of sight, and how
much was due to fear of getting hurt in another relationship. What he did know was that
on a physical level he was able to reach her totally and completely. For now, that was
enough.

He took her in a sweeping drive that caused
her to wrap her arms and legs around him. She
felt a frenzy of love and desire for this man
who seemed to know her body better than she
did. His hands gripped her hips and his mouth
searched hers, daring her to have any secrets
from him.

Once again Elise felt she was out on the lake,
the powerful movements of love simulating the

rocking of the waves. She could feel her body tightening, convulsively clinging to him as he moved deep inside of her until the force of his possession caused her to explode into a million droplets, like the waves breaking on the shore.

Damon shuddered with release and held her tightly in his arms when he rolled over on his back, his chest heaving with the effort to draw air into his lungs. Elise slid to his side and they both drifted off to sleep.

A slight tap on the door some time later aroused them. "Damon?" It was Justin's voice. "Mattie said we'd be eating in about half an hour. Thought I'd let you know."

Elise sat up, for a moment bewildered as to what she was doing in Damon's bed and what time of day it was. The sun was setting, she noticed, and she glanced down at Damon who looked very rested and content.

He ran his hand up and down her back. "Did you sleep well?"

"Fantastic."

"Greatest little sleeping pill there is," he murmured.

"Glad I could oblige," she said tartly.

He laughed. "I could say the same thing, you know. Why are you so defensive about making love with me?"

She shrugged, then realized he couldn't see her. "I'm just not used to behaving like this."

"I know."

Elise glanced at him in surprise. "You do?"

"I may not be able to see you, Elise, but I'm not blind to the person you are. For example, I know you would never have made love to me if you didn't love me."

She could feel the color mounting in her face.

"Isn't that true?"

"Yes."

"Then don't be ashamed of it. As it happens, I also am in love with you. Isn't that great, the way it all worked out?" he said with a grin.

"You make it sound like a game."

"No. But I'm not going to make our coming together something solemn and heavy, either. I feel very fortunate that we met and I was given a chance to get to know you. Once I get my eyesight back, we've got many plans to make. But in the meantime, is there anything wrong in just enjoying each other?"

"No, not really."

"Glad you can see it that way. Now, would you like to pick out something for me to wear tonight?" he asked, sitting up on the side of the bed. "I wonder if dear Cynthia is still here," he muttered.

"You didn't invite her down here?"

"Hardly."

"But she's been here before?"

"Yes. I generally bring a house party with me when I come down here. She came along a couple of times as my hostess."

"Oh."

"Cynthia and I understand each other. Don't let her try to convince you differently. Cynthia is my past—not my present and definitely not my future. All of that is reserved for you."

Elise walked over to the closet and realized she felt a certain freedom since Damon couldn't see her sauntering around the room without clothes. Perhaps by the time his eyesight was restored, she would be more comfortable with the idea. *Now you're beginning to sound like Damon, so sure he'll be able to see again.*

"Are you going to ask her to leave, if she's still here?"

"Not this evening. It must be close to dark by now. Tomorrow will be soon enough."

Elise thought about the coming evening and smiled. For some reason she felt much more comfortable with the idea of spending the evening around Cynthia. It was amazing how reassuring a few hours of lovemaking could be to a person.

She found a caftan in swirling colors and put it on. Matching earrings swung from her ears and she turned around and watched Damon as he completed his own grooming. She had shaved him each morning, but he had learned to brush his hair in a casual style away from his face. Of course the wave immediately fell across his forehead once more.

"Are you ready?" he asked.

"Yes."

He pulled her into his arms. "I love that scent. I always think of you when I smell it. What is it?"

"I don't really know. Mother knows this little old lady back in the hills near her home in Tennessee. She makes perfumes and Mother has always had her make up mine. I'm glad you like it.''

''I knew I'd never smelled it before. It's very special, just as you are to me.''

She gazed into his clear gray eyes. ''You're very special to me, too, Damon. You've taught me so much about myself. Thank you for that.''

''If we don't get out of here right now, I'm not going to be responsible for my actions,'' he said with a grin.

She took his hand and placed it on her arm and together they walked down the hallway to join the world once more.

Ten

Cynthia presided at the end of the table, opposite Damon, and Elise sat on his left, Justin on his right. Elise quietly enjoyed the meal, while Cynthia vivaciously shared anecdotes of her social life, filling Damon in on the activities that had occurred since he'd left Chicago.

Justin sat back and observed. It didn't take much imagination to guess how Damon and Elise had spent the remainder of their afternoon. They both glowed, with love, with good health and with rest. He hadn't minded entertaining Cynthia in Damon's absence; it was just one more way to help out where he could. But the woman herself left him cold.

Not that she hadn't tried to charm him. She'd made it clear that she was more than willing to remain at the lake and keep him company until he explained that he was leaving the next morning for Chicago himself.

"How much longer do you intend to stay down here, Damon?" Cynthia asked with a lilt to her voice. Delicately sipping from her wineglass, she stared at him with an inquiring expression.

It's really too bad he can't see the look of solicitous concern on her face, Elise thought. She glanced over at Justin and was surprised when he winked at her, his eyes darting back to look at Cynthia.

"I'm returning to the hospital in a few weeks and they're going to run some more tests on my eyes, to see when surgery can be scheduled."

"You poor darling. Can't you see anything?"

"No."

"But you get around so well!"

"Thanks to Elise."

Cynthia smiled at Elise. "Yes. And I want to add *my* thanks for your care of him. He's been so fortunate to have someone so capable, and so willing, to look after him."

Damon choked on his drink.

"Be careful, darling," Cynthia admonished. "We can't have anything happening to you now, after you're doing so much better."

Justin decided it was time to change the subject and he asked Cynthia something that led her to another lively discourse regarding life in Chicago.

Damon could see that it was going to be a rather long evening. As long as he'd known Cynthia, he'd never seen this side of her. The woman was a barracuda and he only hoped that Elise wouldn't feel threatened by her presence. He had shown her in every way he knew how that Cynthia meant nothing to him, whereas Elise meant the world to him.

After dinner they sat on the terrace and watched the boats go by, the red and green lights moving ghostlike through the night. During a lull in the conversation, Justin spoke quietly to Damon. "I put Cynthia's things in the spare bedroom. Hope that was all right."

"Certainly. She couldn't leave tonight anyway."

"Do you want me to arrange for her to leave with me in the morning?"

"Yes."

Short and to the point, Justin thought with a slight smile. A little of Cynthia was certainly going a long way.

Justin waited until another lull in the conversation before he stood and stretched. "It's after eleven. I think I'll turn in since I've got to make an early start in the morning."

"Good idea, Justin." Damon stood up. "Why don't you ride back with Justin tomorrow, Cynthia? I'm sure he'd appreciate the company."

The silence on the terrace became electric. Cynthia glared at Elise, who dropped her eyes and gazed at Cynthia's hands. They were clutched in her lap.

"You're more than welcome to come with me," Justin coaxed quietly.

Cynthia forced a smile to her face. "What time do you intend to leave?"

"Whatever would be convenient for you," he responded gallantly.

She sighed. "I'll try to be ready by nine."

"Fine," he said in a relieved tone. "Good night, then."

Cynthia glanced over at Damon. "I'd like to speak with you alone if I might, Damon."

Elise stood up quickly, but Damon grabbed her hand. "There's no reason for you to leave, Elise. Whatever Cynthia cares to say to me can be said in front of you as well."

But Damon couldn't see the pain in Cynthia's eyes—and Elise could. "I'm really very tired, Damon. You should have no trouble finding your way back inside."

He smiled. "True. All right, love. I'll be in there shortly."

After Elise had gone, Damon and Cynthia sat there in the silence of the night. Finally Damon asked, "What did you want to say, Cynthia?"

"I wanted to ask you why?"

"I don't know what you're talking about."

"Why have you taken up with her? I thought you and I had a wonderfully satisfying relationship. What happened?"

Damon heard the pain in her voice and mentally cursed himself. Why hadn't he seen this coming?

"Cynthia, did I ever make any promises to you?"

"No," was her barely audible response.

"We had some good times together. I have enjoyed your company many times in the past. But I can't be possessed. You know that."

"Does she?"

"That's irrelevant. It has never been my intention to hurt you. I'm not even sure that I have. I believe you're trying to make a drama out of this, and it's unnecessary."

"It never mattered to you that I loved you, did it?"

"You hid it well."

"Yes. Because I knew if I ever let you see how I felt, I'd lose you."

Silence greeted her remark.

"I was right, wasn't I?"

More silence.

"I can't help but feel sorry for your innocent little nurse, who no doubt expects all sorts of promises from you."

"She has nothing to do with this."

"No, she probably doesn't. You didn't even let me know you were planning to come down here—before you had the accident. You just left—with no word to me."

"That's right."

"I wonder if you're ever going to know how it feels to love someone so much, then have them walk out of your life without a backward glance?"

Once again, Damon remained silent.

Cynthia stood up. "All right, Damon. I'll go back home tomorrow. I wish you luck. I have a feeling you're going to need it." She walked over to the sliding glass doors and went inside.

Damon sat out on the terrace for a long time, thinking about his conversation with Cynthia, and about Elise. What had happened to him where Elise was concerned? She had wiped everyone else out of his mind. Did it have to do with his accident?

He had even thought that by making love to her he would be rid of his obsession with her, but the lovemaking had only intensified his feelings. Damon felt as though he'd been wandering the face of the earth, looking for something, not knowing what it was he was seeking until Elise appeared in his life. Then he felt as though he had found home, the place for his heart to rest and be comforted.

Facing death had caused him to face his priorities as well. As much as he enjoyed his business, it no longer held the magnetism it once did. What had been his purpose for amassing a fortune? Had Elise been right? Had he wanted power? Then more power? He wasn't sure he even liked the man he had turned into and he wasn't at all sure that Elise would want any part of that person.

He felt so differently now. As though none of his former life really mattered anymore. What mattered was Elise. What mattered was being able to see again, so that she wouldn't be hampered by his lack of sight. He hoped the tests coming up gave the go-ahead to the surgery. He felt so trapped in the darkness.

Damon got up and went inside, snapping the lock behind him. With measured steps he followed the hallway to his bedroom. The door was closed and he opened it softly. He held his breath, listening. Approaching the bed he paused, then let out a sigh of relief. He heard her soft breathing and knew she had joined him. He hadn't been sure she would. Damon couldn't remember ever having been so unsure of himself with anyone as he was around her.

Silently he removed his clothes and quietly crawled into bed next to her. She murmured something and turned so that she was facing him. He pulled her closer to his body, loving the feel of her, treasuring the moment, praying that their future would bring many such moments together.

Elise woke up sometime during the night and realized that Damon had come to bed while she slept. Her back was nestled to his chest and he had an arm and leg over her, so that she couldn't move even if she had any desire to leave.

He appeared to be deeply asleep, his hand cupped around her breast in a familiar position. She was pleased that he was sleeping so well. Her job was done. There had been no reason for her to stay during this past week. He no longer needed to be looked after, or cared for, but since she had arranged to take three weeks and he had made no suggestion that she should leave, she had stayed.

What was it she expected from their relationship? Guy had been the only other man in her life, and after the marriage was over Elise had no desire to form another relationship. And yet, here she was, obviously involved in another relationship. Was she ready for one? Not really. She only knew that her feelings for Damon Trent had been stronger than anything she had ever felt for anyone, Guy included.

How strange to discover that Guy had not been the love of her life, as she had always thought. What they had shared had been fun, but they had never known the closeness that she and Damon had shared—nor the depth. She and Guy had been like children, playing at being married. Damon had shown her how much more there was to share as an adult.

For the first time since Elise had discovered what Guy was really like, she found herself thanking him for being who and what he was and for allowing her to discover for herself that he wasn't what she wanted in life, so that she could gain freedom from the relationship.

Damon's hand tightened for a moment and she held her breath. She realized she was lying on his other arm and he shifted, turning her to face him.

From the faint light coming into the room she studied his face. His eyes were closed and he looked relaxed, but there was a smile on his lips that she didn't believe was caused by a dream, particularly not when his hand lifted her chin and his mouth found hers.

She didn't know if he'd been dreaming or not, but his kiss was filled with passion and she felt as though she'd just been set afire. Her nightgown was around her waist and his hand slid down between them, stroking her abdomen and parting her thighs. Without breaking the contact of the kiss, Damon rolled, putting her on top of him. His hands lifted her hips slightly, fitting her to him, pulling her back down to encase him.

He pulled his mouth away slightly from hers, took a breath, then found her mouth once again. She loved the feel of him inside her, loved the joy of his possession, the wonder of their coming together. It was never the same, but the wondrous magic seemed to spin a web of ecstasy over and around them time after time.

Damon eased her up until her breast was at his mouth and his tongue teased at the nipple, rolling it around in his mouth until Elise thought she would cry out in response to the sensation he was causing.

Although he was underneath her, Damon controlled their coming together, guiding her hips in their rhythm, moving his mouth from first one nipple, then the other, orchestrating, creating, mesmerizing until Elise felt as though she were being lifted high into the heavens, floating with him.

"Now, love! Right now!" His arms wrapped around her convulsively and she felt her body contract rhythmically around him.

"I can't believe this," he finally muttered a few minutes later.

"Believe what?"

"How you affect me. I'm too old for this!"

She smoothed her hand across his damp brow. "And who was it who started this, anyway?"

"Not me," he muttered. "I was just sleeping, minding my own business, when this wildcat leaped on top of my poor, defenseless body...."

She laughed. Elise couldn't help it. He sounded so innocent and so taken advantage of. Moving away from him slightly, she stretched out by his side, enjoying the view of his lean, muscular body. "Well, you won't have to worry about it much longer. Nurse Brandon will be back in St. Louis very shortly."

Her comment caused his smile to disappear. "What are you talking about?"

Surprised at the change in his tone, she said, "I need to be back to work by this weekend. I thought you realized that."

"I don't even know what day it is, or the date. How could I know?"

"I should leave here no later than Friday. This is Wednesday."

"Oh." They lay there together in silence. Elise was drifting off to sleep once more when Damon suddenly spoke. "Don't go, Elise."

"I have to. I have a job."

"I thought you'd be with me when I had my surgery."

"If you have your surgery in St. Louis, I probably will be somewhere nearby."

"I may fly to New York. That's where the specialist is."

"I can't possibly go to New York."

"You could if you quit your job."

"I have no intention of quitting my job."

"I see."

I doubt it, she thought wearily. He had no conception of what it was to live on a salary, to worry about bills, to wonder if she could make everything stretch. The proceeds she received from the sale of the house had gone into savings and she had no intention of touching them. But regardless of how much she loved him, Elise knew that she couldn't rely on a future with Damon. Her few weeks there at the lake were a dream out of time, out of context with her real life.

He had taught her so much and she was grateful. But she had no intention of wishing for what she couldn't have—a life with him.

Damon felt so damned frustrated. He wanted to marry her, but not unless his surgery was a success. She loved him. He knew she did, but he wasn't going to ask her to look after him in the event that he was permanently blind.

So she was leaving in a couple of days. He could handle that. He would have to handle it and hope the surgery could be scheduled soon. He hated to think of the bleak days ahead without her.

Elise woke up alone the next morning. As there were no sounds coming from the bathroom, she realized that Damon must be already up and dressed. She stretched, wondering what to plan for the day.

A slight tap at the door caught her attention. "Come in."

The door opened and Cynthia walked in, looking chic and expensive. "I couldn't leave without telling you goodbye," she said in a chatty voice, her eyes quickly taking in the signs of Elise's occupancy in the room. She walked over to the dresser where Elise had left the few cosmetics that she wore.

Picking up the unusually shaped crystal atomizer sitting there, she said, "What in the world is this?"

"Perfume."

Cynthia sprayed some liberally around her and said, "Not quite my thing. Too floral."

Elise remained silent, waiting for the woman to leave.

Cynthia looked at Elise through the mirror. "Surely you don't think he's going to stay with you any longer than he did with me?"

"Whatever I think, it's none of your business."

"Yes, I know. I don't know what it is about women. We always think we're going to be the exception, the one to cause a man to change. And we're always shocked and upset when we find that he is still the man we first met and fell in love with." She quit playing with the small vials and bottles and turned to face Elise.

"Enjoy him, but don't try to hang on to him. You notice that I'm not trying to fight his decision. I know better. Damon can be ruthless, but I know you haven't seen that side of him. Pray that you never do."

Elise stood up. "If you'll excuse me, I really need to shower and get dressed."

Cynthia nodded her head. "Of course. Justin and I will be leaving in a few moments. I'm glad we could have this little talk."

I just bet you are, Elise thought, watching the door close behind the woman. But she had also seen her pain and knew that her remarks carried a great deal of truth. Elise recognized that she was totally out of her league with these people. Her background and her marriage had not prepared her to bid the high stakes necessary to stay in the game. She had already lost her heart. She only hoped she could hang on to her dignity and her sanity.

Elise showered and dressed within a few minutes and decided to step outside through the bedroom door onto the terrace. She wasn't ready to talk to anyone just yet, particularly not Damon.

However, when she walked over to the edge she realized he was already outside, and had followed the path down to the shore. *This is one time I'm glad he can't see me,* she decided with a grim smile. *I'm not ready to face him.*

Elise was around the corner from the terrace where they usually had breakfast. She heard Cynthia and Justin talking, then watched as Cynthia started down the path toward Damon.

As she approached him he suddenly looked up and smiled, a warm, loving smile that drove a dagger through Elise's heart. She watched the scene unfold before her as though it were in slow motion: Cynthia in her colorful slacks and camisole top, standing on the step just above Damon so that she appeared taller than she was, Damon sensing her presence and facing her, his arms reaching for her as he said, "Good morning, darling. I've missed you." He pulled her to him in a possessive grasp that caused a sudden rush of nausea to hit Elise's stomach and she spun around, dashing back into the bedroom.

As soon as his lips touched hers, Damon knew the woman in his arms wasn't Elise. But how could that be? She wore Elise's unique scent. His arms slipped away, and he recognized the smaller build. "Cynthia."

She laughed, a little uncertainly. "Who did you think it was?"

"Why are you wearing Elise's perfume?"

Until that moment, she'd forgotten about spraying the light floral scent over her. "Oh, I was just seeing if I liked it, but I'm afraid it's just not me."

Damon felt a rage so fierce that for a moment he thought he might strike the woman in front of him. And it wasn't even her fault. She had no idea that Elise's perfume had always let him know whenever she was nearby. All those weeks in the hospital, all she had had to do was open the door, and the breeze would waft her scent to him.

"Where *is* Elise?" he asked, his temper on a tight rein.

Cynthia glanced around. "She was going to take a shower and get dressed when I saw her last. I told her goodbye."

He nodded. "Where is Justin?"

"He said he'd meet me in front. Damon, will I see you again?"

"Come on, Cynthia, don't be so damned dramatic. Of course we'll see each other."

She leaned over and kissed his cheek. "Take care of yourself. I hope the surgery turns out all right."

"So do I," he muttered, still irritated at how easily he could be fooled.

"Do you need any help getting back to the terrace?"

"No! I'm fine. Don't keep Justin waiting. You've got a long trip ahead of you."

"Goodbye, Damon."

"Bye, Cynthia. Give your father my regards."

Damon waited where he was, listening to the click of Cynthia's shoes against the stone walkway. He heard the car pull out of the drive, and the quick horn honk that was Justin's signal saying goodbye. Eventually, Damon returned to the terrace where Mattie offered him more coffee.

"Has Elise eaten?"

"She said she wasn't hungry."

"Oh. Where is she?"

"I haven't seen her for a while. Do you want me to find her for you?"

"No. She's on vacation. There's no reason for her to hover over me." *Except that I miss her and I want to be with her.*

Sometime later Mattie returned. "Elise asked to borrow my car. Said she had some errands to run and to tell you she'd be back later."

He wondered why she didn't tell him she was leaving? Was she feeling pressured perhaps? He tried to think back to their conversation of the night before but the mental pictures of their lovemaking kept getting in the way.

She was so totally open and giving with him whenever they made love. But she wasn't ready to commit her life to him. Not that he had asked for that, but he wondered if she was concerned about his possible blindness. She had never mentioned it, but then, being a nurse she probably wouldn't want to upset him with any negative comments.

Damon sighed. If they could just get through the next few weeks, everything would be fine.

Eleven

It was almost midnight when Elise pulled into the driveway in front of the house. She felt quite pleased that she had found her way back without getting lost. Of course she had watched her turns leaving and had received instructions from Mattie.

The house was dark, which wasn't surprising, although she had assumed Mattie would leave a light on for her. She had called her to see if she would mind her using the car for a while longer. Mattie had encouraged her to take her time. It was the first time she'd left

Damon's property alone during the time they had been down there.

She had needed the time away and had used it to buy souvenirs for her family and friends. Eventually she had found a seafood restaurant that overlooked the lake and had lingered there, enjoying the view until dark. Later she had driven to the dam and parked nearby, watching the stream of people and traffic visiting the area. There was such a festive air about the place. She wondered if the Las Vegas strip looked anything like that, with the neon lights flashing and the sound of live music coming from many of the places.

Luckily the front door of Damon's home had been left unlocked for her and she slipped inside, closing it softly behind her. She had decided to sleep in her old room so as not to disturb Damon. Elise was almost through the living area when his voice suddenly spoke from the darkened room.

"Where have you been?"

"Damon! You startled me. I thought you'd be asleep by now."

"Where have you been?" he repeated.

"Didn't Mattie tell you? I decided to have dinner out."

"That was hours ago."

"Then I did some sight-seeing."

"After dark?"

"Damon, what is this? This is the first day I've had to myself since we came down here. Why the third degree?" She walked over and opened the blinds, letting in the moonlight. When she turned around she could see him sitting in the large chair by the fireplace.

"Did it ever occur to you that I might worry? You don't know the area. You could have gotten lost—"

"But I didn't. I found my way back just fine."

"A woman alone isn't safe after dark anywhere, Elise. You know that."

"There were always plenty of people around."

"What's wrong?" he probed.

"Nothing's wrong. I just feel like a child standing here answering all your questions." He still sat there, waiting. "Look. I'm tired and I'd like to get some sleep. Can we save this until in the morning?"

"Save what?"

"Whatever it is. I don't know, myself."

Damon stood up and came toward the sound of her voice. "I missed you today, love." He started to put his arms around her and she jerked away.

"Don't!"

"Have I become a leper now, you don't want me touching you?"

"I'm just tired, that's all."

"I may be blind, Elise, but I'm not stupid. Something's wrong. I can hear it in your voice, feel it when I touch you. Has something upset you?"

She started down the hall. "I'd rather not discuss it tonight." Opening the door to the room she had used during the first two weeks she had been there, Elise quickly entered, turned back the covers and began to remove her clothes. She would sleep in her panties and bra. Nothing could coax her to go into Damon's bedroom that night.

Damon must have gone into his room because she heard him call her. "Elise? Dammit, where are you?" She heard the pain and frustration in his voice and decided that playing hide-and-seek with a blind man did not become her.

She walked to the door of her bedroom. "I'm here, Damon."

"What the hell are you doing in there?" He walked down the hall toward her.

"I prefer to sleep in here tonight."

"All right. I understand. You're upset. Was it something I said or did? Was it something that Cynthia said or did? She told me she'd stopped in to say goodbye to you this morning. Did she say something to upset you?"

"No. She said nothing that I didn't already know."

"And what's that supposed to mean?"

"That you aren't known for your long-lasting relationships."

Damn the woman. If Cynthia were here right now, I'd wring her neck. "That's true. You're the first."

Elise smiled. "I hardly think that a few weeks together makes our relationship long-lasting, Damon."

"I mean, you're the first woman with whom I've ever wanted to share a permanent relationship."

She couldn't believe it. Here was another man who expected her to overlook his other relationships. Was she doomed to fall in love with the same type of male, or were they all that way?

Elise felt at least a hundred years old—weighted down. "I'm sorry, Damon. That's not what I want."

He reached out and touched her cheek with his hand as though needing the physical contact. "You mean you were looking for a vacation affair? Were you planning to forget all about me when you returned to St. Louis?"

As if she could ever forget him. Elise recognized that the few months she had shared with Damon had made a more lasting impression on her than the eight years she had shared with Guy. Time had nothing to do with the depth of her feelings.

"Does it matter?" she asked wearily.

"You're damned right it matters! I love you. If my surgery works out I intend to marry you! How can you ask whether it matters or not?"

"Damon, I have no intention of marrying anyone, ever. I had no idea that you were even thinking of marriage or I would have told you. Actually, I thought you knew that."

"You can't hold every man responsible for your former husband's behavior, Elise. I had nothing to do with that."

"I know. But at least Guy never brought his other girlfriends around where I had to see him with them, watch him kiss them—" Her voice suddenly failed her, as pain formed a knot in her throat.

"You saw me with Cynthia this—"

"Yes," she interrupted. "But it doesn't matter. I have no reason to complain and I'm not."

"Dammit, Elise. I thought she was you!"

Now *that* was original. She wondered how long it had taken him to think that one up.

"She was wearing your perfume."

"What has that got to do with it?"

"Everything! Don't you understand? It was your perfume that identified you to me every time you walked into my room, either at the hospital or here. It is so distinctively you. It never occurred to me that anyone else would be wearing it. Why should it? You told me your mother had it made especially for you!"

Flashbacks of Damon's early days in the hospital came back to her. She had wondered at the time how he recognized her. It was possible he was telling the truth. But was she willing to base her future on that possibility? Was she willing to trust another man?

"It really doesn't matter, Damon. I have no intention of marrying you. I never have." She pulled away from him. "If you'll excuse me, I'd like to go to bed."

"At least sleep with me."

"No. That wasn't a very wise choice in the first place. I had finally gotten used to sleeping alone after eight years. Now I'll have to get used to it all over again." She glanced up at his shadow in the doorway. "Good night, Damon." She went into the bathroom, closing the door behind her.

Her knees felt weak and she moved over to the side of the tub and sat down. Elise realized that she had never turned on a light since coming back that night. Damon wasn't aware of the lack of light and her eyes had become adjusted to the dark. She had no desire to face herself in the mirror at the moment and she continued to sit there in the dark, waiting for him to leave her bedroom.

How could she have been so stupid as to have made love to him in the first place? But she knew. To her, loving someone meant wanting to express that love in its most ultimate sense. Of course men treated it differently. That was why so many misunderstandings occurred.

Now she had to pay the price for her folly. Had she never made love to him, she was certain it would have been easier to forget him. But forget him she would.

The next morning Elise found Damon sitting on the terrace drinking coffee. For just a moment she allowed herself the luxury of watching him. A light breeze played with his hair, causing it to flicker across his brow. The light caught the gray in his eyes and they flashed silver when he turned his head in her direction.

"Good morning."

She knew she had made no sound, but the same playful breeze that had flirted with Damon must have brought the scent of her perfume to him. Perhaps he had told her the truth about yesterday. It really didn't matter.

She sat down across from him. "Did you sleep well?" she asked politely.

"What do you think?"

He had shadows under his eyes and there were faint lines around them, similar to the ones she had seen in the mirror that morning.

Mattie brought her coffee and left a carafe on the table. Elise sipped the hot liquid, wondering what to say. Then Damon saved her the trouble.

"I've decided to go back to St. Louis today. You intended to leave tomorrow anyway, didn't you?"

"Yes."

"I called the hospital this morning and they're willing to run the tests in the morning."

"And if they decide to operate?"

"I'll know more about that tomorrow." He set his mug down. "Would you mind driving me back?"

"Not at all."

"Thank you. I didn't want to bother Justin if it could be avoided. He's in the middle of some delicate negotiations."

"I understand."

Never had Damon felt quite so helpless. She sounded so polite, and so distant. He leaned forward. "Elise, please don't make any decisions about us until after my surgery. That's all I ask. There's a chance we won't need to make any decisions."

"Stop it! Whether you can see or not see has absolutely nothing to do with my feelings about you, and it certainly wouldn't stop me from marrying you!"

A slight smile hovered around his lips. Gone were the aloofness and the politeness. At least he had found some emotions. "Then what is stopping you?"

"I refuse to place myself in a vulnerable position again, where I am forced to trust another human being. It's too painful and I refuse to go through life wondering if they're telling the truth, wondering if I'm being lied to. I don't intend to ever live that way again!"

"Do you think I have lied to you?"

"I have no idea. I don't care."

"You know, Elise, as many times as I have cursed my inability to see, I at least recognized my blindness for what it was and attempted to function around it. You, on the other hand, embrace your blindness, clutch it like a drowning person, determined to go through life handicapped, refusing to see what life has to offer you."

"Pain and suffering, betrayal, heartache. Believe me, I've tried them all and I don't think I'll miss a thing by giving them up."

"Elise, I have never lied to you. I never intend to. You have my word on the matter. I love you. I'd marry you tomorrow if it were possible. I never believed I would meet anyone to whom I could say that. It's ironic that I have never even seen you, and that there's a definite possibility I never will. Part of that is up to you." He reached for her hand and folded it within his own. "I really believe that you love me. You've shown me in too many ways for me to believe differently. Yet you're afraid to trust me. I can understand that, too. There are no guarantees in this life, my love. No certainties. Neither of us may live to see tomorrow. And what a shame it would be if for whatever time we have, feeling the way we do about each other, we did not spend it together."

Elise was silent. He could play on her emotions like a master. How could she resist? But she remembered the pain of seeing him with Cynthia and knew that the longer she stayed with him, shared his life with him, the harder it would be to let him go at some later point. As he'd said, there were no guarantees.

"When do you want to leave?"

Her quiet question convinced him that nothing he could say would change her mind.

"As soon as you can pack."

"I'll be ready within the hour." Elise got up and went into the house, into Damon's room, and began to gather her things.

She refused to look at the bed, to remember the shared intimacies. She knew she was doing the right thing for her. She was willing to give up the ecstasy in order not to face the possible despair. She was willing to continue her life in a quiet existence without the fulfillment of her heart's desire or the possible loss of that same desire.

Full of advice and cheerful warnings, Mattie waved them off with a big smile, reminding Damon to have someone call her regarding his surgery.

"She's a neat lady," Elise said, pulling away from the house.

"Yes, she is. I'm fortunate to have found her."

"Does she live here year-round?"

"Yes."

"I wonder if she ever gets lonely."

"Loneliness is a state of mind, Elise. Surely you know that."

She smiled a little sadly. "I suppose I never gave it much thought. But you're right."

Damon leaned back and closed his eyes. He had never realized how lonely he had been until he'd met Elise. Now that she was leaving his life, he couldn't begin to comprehend the hole that was going to be left there. But how could he blame her? She had just as much right not to choose to be with him as he had the right to choose to be with her.

How ironic that none of his money or power could get him what he most wanted in the world—Elise's love and trust.

They drove directly to the hospital and Damon was admitted once more. As soon as he was settled Elise took a taxi home to her apartment.

Never had it seemed so small and cheerless. Had she really lived there all these months without noticing? She already wondered what the results of Damon's tests would be. After unpacking everything she tried to reach her mother, but there was no answer. She couldn't remember when they were due home from Italy. For that matter, they could all have decided to change their plans and stay longer!

While she lay in bed that night, unable to sleep, she repeated to herself, "Remember . . . today is the beginning of the rest of your life. Make the most of it."

And why did the memory of Damon suddenly pop into her head? *Please, dear God, return his sight to him.* She thought about her prayer for a few moments, then added, *And if you could see your way clear to helping me find the ability to trust a man again, I'd appreciate it.*

That was all it would take. The ability to trust another person. Was that so impossible? *More like a miracle!*

By the time Elise reported to work on Sunday afternoon, Damon was no longer in the hospital. During her break she went to see his doctor.

"I recommended that he was ready for surgery, Elise. He's made an excellent recovery. I'm more hopeful that the laser surgery will be effective and that he should regain his sight with no problem."

"I'm so glad. He's never allowed himself to face the thought that it might be permanent." She glanced up at the doctor. "Did he go to New York?"

"Yes. I believe they scheduled the surgery for later this week."

And he didn't even let me know. Why should he? Hadn't she made it clear she was no longer a part of his life? Elise returned to ICU, trying to face the fact that it was time to pick up the threads of her life once more.

Justin stood outside Damon's hospital room talking with his surgeon. "How soon will you know?"

"Not until we take the bandages off. Right now his eyes need a chance to heal. I have every reason to believe he'll be fine, but I'm concerned about his emotional condition."

"How's that?"

"For some reason, he doesn't seem to care. When I examined him a few months ago in St. Louis I felt a real energy emanating from him, a driving force that seems to be missing now. It's as though he's given up."

"I'll talk to him, if you think that will help."

"I have no idea. Does he have any family? Anyone he'd like to have here with him?"

Justin pictured Elise as he'd last seen her, sitting on the terrace with Damon, her hand resting in his, her eyes sparkling as she listened to him. Oh, yes, he could think of

someone, but Damon had made it clear he
didn't want her contacted. Justin didn't know
what had happened between them and it
wasn't his place to interfere.

"I can't think of anyone," he finally answered.

"Well, see what you can do. It doesn't make
much sense to me. From his original injuries I
wouldn't have expected him to pull through at
all and he came out of the anesthetic fighting
for his life. Yet now that he's so nearly recovered, and the prognosis is good for his eyesight, he seems to have given up."

"He's been fighting a long time. Perhaps
he's tired."

"Maybe so." He patted the younger man on
the shoulder. "See what you can do. I've done
all I can."

Twelve

The cold north wind swept the fall leaves before it, and Elise's pace quickened. She had worn a light jacket when she left the apartment that morning, thinking that the day would grow warmer, but it hadn't.

She shifted her shopping bag to her left hand and reached for her apartment key. Turning the lock and pushing inside, she gratefully placed the bag on the table near the entryway and closed the door.

November was certainly starting off with a great deal of cool weather. She hung up her jacket and made some coffee, hoping to remove the chill from her bones. Memories of the summer and her stay at the lake flooded over her.

Almost four months had passed since she'd seen or heard from Damon. She had never heard if his surgery had been successful. On more than one occasion she had picked up the phone to call his office in Chicago. Justin had given her the number months ago in case she needed to reach him while Damon was so ill. One time she had actually dialed the number, but when she heard the cheerful voice answer, "Good afternoon, Trent Enterprises," she had hung up without answering.

What was there to say? *I was thinking about you, so thought I'd call?* That wouldn't be a lie. He was always on her mind. How about, *Hi there, thought I'd call to see if you're still blind.*

He had told her *she* was blind. At the time she hadn't understood what he meant, but as the months had passed she began to see how much she had been willing to leave out of her life for fear of being hurt.

Elise poured a cup of coffee and wandered into the living room. She had the next two days off and had already done all of her shopping and cleaning. Staring out the window she absently noted how many brown leaves still clung to the trees, refusing to let go.

Was that what she was doing—clinging to the past, refusing to let go?

The phone rang, a brash sound in the silence, causing her to flinch and almost spill her coffee. Placing the cup on the small table by her favorite chair, she sat down and picked up the phone.

"Hello?"

"Elise? Hi, this is Guy."

She hadn't talked to Guy since last summer and she was surprised to hear from him.

"Hi, yourself. How's business?" She was surprised to hear the light, cheerful note in her voice. Suddenly she discovered she was actually glad to hear from him.

He sounded just as surprised at his reception. His voice came over the wire with more of a bounce. "Actually, business couldn't be better. I just finished putting a tour package together for late next spring to tour the Canadian Rockies.''

"Sounds great."

"Yes . . . so how have you been?''

"About the same. Working, coming home, working, etc.''

"How's your mom and Melanie?''

"Oh, they're fine. Mel started to college this fall. They went to Europe over the summer.''

"No kidding. I didn't think anything would pry your mom away from home.''

She laughed. "Neither did I, but Italy proved to be an irresistible lure. Mel said they had to talk her into coming home. I think she would have moved over there with any encouragement at all.'' Elise had taken a long weekend and gone down to see her mother and sister after they'd returned home. Never had she seen her mother looking better, and Melanie had been full of stories about the gorgeous men in Italy.

"Uh, Elise . . .''

"Yes?''

"I wanted to let you know that . . . I asked Merrilee to move out a few weeks ago.''

"I see." Her tone was carefully neutral, but she realized that she really didn't care.

"I couldn't handle her jealousy. It was strange, but once she moved in she tried to take over my life. I got the third degree every time I walked through the door. She always knew my schedule and called me every day I was on the road, demanding to know what I'd been doing and who I'd been seeing."

Elise didn't know what to say so she didn't respond.

"And I remembered how it was with us, you and me, and I hated myself for spoiling what we had."

"Don't, Guy. There's no point in going through all of that again."

"I know. It's been a year since you left, you know."

"Yes, I know."

"What I wanted to tell you was that none of it had anything to do with you. I mean, the way I acted on the road didn't take anything away from what I shared with you. You know how much I enjoy people and how I like to kid around. Well, I'd be kidding around and suddenly discover that I'd talked myself into a corner. I was afraid I'd look stupid if I tried to backtrack and pretend that they had misunderstood. It was a lot easier to go along with the situation, knowing there was no way you would find out. But I hated what I was doing, and when I recognized I was too weak to change my behavior, I hated myself even more.''

"Guy, there's no reason for you to tell me all of this.''

"I felt that there was because I thought you were blaming yourself, just as I tried to blame you for what I was doing. But it wasn't you. It was never you, babe. I just never appreciated what I had until I lost it.''

The soft hum of the telephone wire was the only sound.

"You'd probably laugh to know that I'm not seeing anyone now. Now that I'm single and with no ties I find that I'm spending more time alone than I ever did before, trying to decide what I want out of life, where I'm headed.''

"I know the feeling,'' Elise managed to say.

"Yeah, well, I wasn't the greatest husband in the world but I wanted you to know that if you ever need me, for anything at all, for someone to talk to, throw things at, whatever, I'm here. You will always have a very special place in my heart.''

"Thank you, Guy. I appreciate your telling me."

"Yeah, well, look, I've got to get back to work. So give me a call one of these days. Maybe we can get together for dinner or something. How about it?''

"I just might do that, Guy. You never can tell.''

"Take care, babe.''

"You, too, Guy. Thanks for calling.''

Elise hung up the phone and stared out the window once more. She really was thankful he had called. She hadn't realized how much she had changed until she heard his voice again and discovered it was no longer painful to hear from him.

She had expected so much from their relationship. Too much, perhaps? Had either one of them been prepared for marriage and all that it entailed, or had they only seen the happily ever after that was supposedly promised?

Her thoughts returned to Damon. She had always known exactly where she stood with him. He had said that he wanted to marry her, but only if his eyesight was restored.

She wondered how he felt about her now. She glanced at her watch. It was after four o'clock. On impulse, she picked up the phone and dialed from memory his Chicago office number. She heard two rings, then a voice.

"Good afternoon, Trent Enterprises."

"May I speak to Mr. Trent, please?"

"I'm sorry, Mr. Trent is out of town."

Elise felt her heart sink. "When is he expected to return?"

"Just a moment, and I'll check for you," answered the pleasant voice. Elise heard a click on the line, then music began to play. Only a few bars later the voice returned. "His secretary said he should be in the office no later than three tomorrow afternoon."

Tomorrow. He'd be in Chicago tomorrow. "Thank you," she managed to say and hung up.

She could talk with him tomorrow. She could even *see* him tomorrow, if she had the courage to fly to Chicago. It was less than an hour's flight.

If she were to go, what would she say? Could she tell him she'd changed her mind? That she finally realized that being with him for whatever length of time they could share was more important to her than promises of eternal bliss? That given the choice of being safe but only half alive or being with him and being totally alive, she was opting for conscious life, instead of unconscious existence?

Would he care to hear it after all these months? There was no way to know in advance, and she had every intention of finding out by meeting him, face-to-face.

Once again Elise picked up the phone, this time to make reservations to fly to Chicago the next day.

It was after four o'clock by the time Elise's taxi deposited her in front of the downtown office building that held Trent Enterprises. She paused in the mammoth marble lobby and checked the directory for the correct floor, then found the bank of elevators that serviced that floor.

When she stepped out of the elevator, Elise paused. Understated luxury surrounded her, from the plush carpeting to the richly paneled walls and original oil paintings. Several green plants were scattered about the area, giving a feeling of freshness to the room. A well-groomed receptionist smiled, and in a pleasant voice that Elise recognized from their phone conversation asked,

"May I help you?"

"I would like to see Damon Trent, please."

"One moment." She picked up the phone and pushed a button. A moment later she said, "There's a lady here to see Mr. Trent." After listening for another moment, she hung up and said with a smile, "If you'll follow the hallway to the end door, his secretary will be able to help you."

Her heart sank. His secretary. Of course he would have his callers screened. She should have known that. Elise had never tried to picture Damon as the head of his own business, not a business as large as this, anyway. She almost turned around and left, but was too embarrassed to do so in front of the friendly receptionist.

She started down the hallway. Before she reached the closed door it opened and a woman watched her come closer. The woman was probably in her early fifties, very well groomed, and appeared to be extremely businesslike and efficient. But of course. Damon would tolerate nothing less.

When Elise paused at the door, the woman stepped back with a smile and motioned her inside.

In a carefully modulated voice, she asked, "Do you have an appointment with Mr. Trent?"

"No, I'm afraid I don't." There was a slight tremor in her voice and she cleared her throat.

His secretary gave her a quizzical smile. "What is your name?"

"Elise Brandon."

She caught a slight flicker of expression on the woman's face, but then it was gone and she decided she must have imagined it. "If you'll have a seat, Ms. Brandon, I'll tell Mr. Trent you're here."

The woman walked around the desk and picked up the phone, pushing a button. Elise sat down. Her knees were shaking so much she

had wondered how much longer they would
support her. She had been crazy to come, crazy
to fly here on the off chance she could see him.
No doubt his secretary was notifying the
building security right at that moment.

"I'm sorry to disturb you, Mr. Trent," Elise
heard his secretary say, "Elise Brandon is here
to see you." Elise watched the woman for any
change of expression, but her face remained
calm and professional while she listened to his
reply. She nodded. "Certainly, Mr. Trent."

She placed the phone back on its receiver,
then looked at Elise with a warm smile. "You
may go in, Ms. Brandon." She gestured to the
door to her right.

He was going to see her. He was there and he
had agreed for her to come in. She stood up
shakily, then raising her chin ever so slightly,
she nodded. "Thank you."

When she passed her desk Elise could have
sworn she heard his secretary whisper, "Thank
you, Ms. Brandon!"

Elise pushed the door open. It made no
sound. From her vantage point by the door,
the room looked as long as a football field.
Two walls were glass, tinted a rich golden color

that lit up the area like the inside of a Christmas tree ornament. The same plush carpeting muffled her footsteps as she approached the oversize desk and the man who stood behind it, facing the back window.

The view was spectacular—Lake Michigan glistened in the bright rays of the sun, Lake Shore Drive edged the water like a necklace.

"Hello, Damon."

He turned around and the first thing she noticed was his dark glasses. *Oh, no! The surgery didn't help!* She really wasn't prepared, she discovered. Like Damon, she had been convinced, because he was so positive, that the surgery would restore his sight. Now she understood why she had never heard from him.

Her gaze quickly registered Damon, the businessman. His suit was impeccably tailored, but he had lost weight since she had last seen him. His face looked older. There were lines that hadn't been there last summer. His mouth looked as though he'd forgotten how to smile.

"Hello, Elise. Won't you have a seat?" He motioned to the plush chairs arranged in front of his desk, and when she was seated, he sat down in the massive chair behind the desk and leaned back.

"What brings you to Chicago?"

"Impulse."

His left eyebrow climbed so that she saw it behind the dark shades. "Funny, I never saw you as particularly impulsive."

"That's true, I'm not. It's only recently I've discovered how much I've been locked in by my behavior." She stared at him, trying to figure out what he was thinking. "I'm working to change that."

"I see."

There was that phrase again. *I see.* He used it so often. And he was right. He did see— much more than she did, even though she had her eyesight.

"How have you been, Damon?"

"Busy. You know how it is. Business as usual."

"How is Justin?"

His mouth moved into a half smile. "Fine. He's in Florida today and will fly to San Francisco tomorrow. He's taken over much of the traveling I used to do."

Her heart contracted as though a hand had squeezed it.

"Have you been down to the lake recently?" she asked in an attempt to change the subject.

"No."

So much for that. Well, Elise, old girl. Now that you're here, what are you going to tell him?

She took a slow, deep breath, then exhaled equally slowly. "Damon, I came to Chicago because I wanted to see you."

"Why?"

Her eyes pleaded with him but of course he didn't know that. "I realized after you left how much I've been running and hiding from myself and the world. You were right. I have never been happier than I was those few weeks with you at the lake."

He tilted his head slightly as though waiting for more.

"I love you, Damon. And I trust that love. I wanted you to be aware that I trust my feelings now. I've begun to discover who and what I am, and what I want out of life. And most of all, I've discovered that if there's any way possible, I'd like to share my life with you.''

"I appreciate your coming here to tell me. That took courage, I know.''

She smiled. Her heart was still pounding heavily in her chest but she felt lighter than she had in years. No wonder they said that confession was good for the soul. She had just thrown off some burdens that had weighed her down for a long time.

Elise stood up. "Yes, it did. I think I've even managed to surprise myself." Her smile widened. "I know you're busy so I'll let you get back to work." She glanced down at her hand, clenched on the back of the chair on which she had been sitting. "I wish you the very best life has to offer." Her eyes flickered upward and she hurriedly glanced at his face. There was a small smile on his lips. She was pleased to see that, at least. "Goodbye, Damon."

She crossed the large room in silence, glad that he couldn't see her. Tears were running down her cheeks. They were caused by relief at having said to him all she had wanted to say, joy at seeing him again, sorrow that he could not see and a sense of loss that, even with her explanation, he wasn't going to accept what she had to offer. It was too little, too late.

"Elise?" His voice was quiet but she heard him.

She paused at the door, her hand on the doorknob. "Yes?"

"I thought I might spend Thanksgiving at the lake. Would you care to join me?"

She hastily scrubbed at the tears running down her cheeks. His secretary would really wonder about her. She found a handkerchief in her purse and dabbed at her face. Then she turned to face him. "If I can get the time off... yes, I really would."

His smile widened and Elise noticed that his shoulders relaxed. He must have been under a strain, too.

"Why don't you call and let me know."

She nodded, then remembered. "Yes, I'll do that."

"Be careful going home."

"I will. I'm flying. It was too long to drive."

He nodded.

"I hope to see you soon, Damon," she said softly and opened the door, closing it softly behind her.

His secretary was not at her desk, and by the time Elise reached the receptionist she felt better prepared to face another person.

All the way to the airport and later on the plane, Elise thought about spending a few days with Damon. She had been working extra hours as well as holidays for others who had made plans. Surely she would be able to take a few days off.

There was nothing more important than being with Damon again. Absolutely nothing.

Three weeks later Elise sat by the window of her apartment watching the street. She had changed shifts with Diana Fuller and had gotten off at three o'clock because Damon had told her he would be driving and would probably not reach St. Louis until after six o'clock. It was now a quarter to six, according to Elise's watch. She had packed the evening before and now had nothing to do but wait.

Tomorrow was Thanksgiving. After she had called to let him know she would be able to get the time off, Damon had called her a couple of times. He sounded relaxed and casual, interested in her day, but never said anything in the least bit intimate.

What had she expected? Hadn't he made it clear to her that he made no promises he couldn't keep? There had never been promises between them. Not that she needed them. Elise was content to enjoy each day, even each hour, as it came and not to fill her life with unrealistic expectations. It was enough that she would have the next few days with him. A month ago she never expected to see him again.

A long, black limousine turned the corner and headed toward her. She wasn't surprised. Someone would have had to drive him. She couldn't help but wonder if Justin had brought him. It would be nice to see him again.

Elise grabbed her weekender bag and her purse, made sure the door was locked and was out on the curb by the time the car stopped. The driver got out, a young man she had never seen before, and smiled.

"I'll put your bag in the trunk."

The back door opened from within and she stepped inside. Damon sat there with a smile, his dark glasses in place.

"Hello, Damon," Elise murmured a little breathlessly.

When she sat down Damon pulled her over to him, kissing her soundly. "Hello, yourself."

She laughed, a soft, breathless sound. She never knew what to expect from him next!

The driver closed the door behind her, got behind the wheel and they started down the street.

"Did you work today?" he asked.

"Yes. I worked today so I could have Sunday off."

"Fair enough."

"How about you?"

"No, my holiday started this morning when I left Chicago."

"Good for you."

He grinned, a flash of white that caught at her heartstrings. "I've been busy planning our time at the lake."

"Oh, have you?"

"Yes. Mattie is excited that we're coming down."

"I'm looking forward to seeing her."

For the remainder of the trip they talked constantly. Neither brought up his surgery, but it seemed as though every other subject was mentioned. It had been so long since she'd had a lively discussion with someone, shared her thoughts and listened to new ideas.

They laughed together over silly things, and by the time they reached the lake it was hard for her to remember they had ever been apart.

Of course the lake looked different now that the leaves had all turned brown and many of the trees were bare. The oak stand stood stark against the night, with only a few shadows of leaves determined to hang on.

Although it was dark, their arrival was similar to the last time. Mattie was waiting at the door and when they walked inside Elise discovered a table set in front of the fireplace, a small fire dancing merrily.

"I thought you might enjoy a little atmosphere," Mattie explained with a grin.

"Thanks, Mattie," Damon said, giving her a hug. He turned to the driver. "Ms. Brandon's suitcase goes in the guest room on the left," he explained.

Another question answered. They wouldn't be sharing a room.

Much later Elise sat in front of the mirror in her room, brushing out her hair. She had allowed it to grow even longer since summer, and usually wore it in a chignon because it was easier to keep. Unbound, it parted naturally on the side, falling around her face in waves, then tumbling over her shoulders. She remembered how much Damon used to enjoy running his hands through it.

She studied her face. Her eyes sparkled and there was color in her cheeks. The slight tan she still had from the summer was emphasized by her marine-blue nightgown, its deep inset of lace barely concealing her breasts.

It had been almost midnight when Damon suggested they turn in, but she had been too keyed up to sleep. Even after taking a long, soaking bath she had been wide awake, so had decided to brush her hair in hopes of becoming more relaxed.

Damon had removed his glasses earlier in the evening, and she had enjoyed watching his eyes light up with humor. At times they darkened with a deep glow that caused her breathing to become erratic. But other than a rather lingering good-night kiss, he'd made no overtures toward her.

Elise had turned out the lamp and was crawling into bed when she heard a loud crash. It sounded as though it came from the living room.

She darted through the door and down the hallway, flipping on the wall switch when she came to the living room. A couple of lamps came on, causing a soft glow to permeate the room.

Damon stood by the bar, a jumble of glasses lying there.

"Are you okay?" she asked breathlessly.

He laughed. "Other than being hopelessly clumsy, I'm fine," he said as he began to turn around. "I didn't want to disturb you by turning on a light and thought I'd pour myself a drink when—" He stopped talking and stared at her, his gaze taking in her tumbled hair, the sheerness of her gown, the soft curves of her breasts, tiny waist and flaring hips. "My God, Elise, you are the most beautiful woman I have ever seen." His reverent tone shook her until she realized the implications of what he was saying.

"Damon! You can see!"

He looked puzzled. "Of course I can see."

"But you never said. And I thought...I mean...you wear dark glasses...."

"I wear dark glasses because my eyes are still very light sensitive, although the doctor said that should clear up eventually. They also get tired easily, so I try not to read much as yet." He paused, recognizing her shock. "You mean all this time you thought I was blind?"

"Of course. You didn't say anything that would cause me to believe any differently."

"Yet it didn't stop you from coming down here with me."

"No. I'm so happy for you that you can see, but it doesn't change how I feel about you."

He walked over to her, his forefinger stroking her cheek. "And how is that, love?"

"You know how I feel about you. I love you."

"Enough to marry me?"

"Yes."

"No matter what might happen in the future?"

"Yes."

"Oh, Elise," he said, pulling her into his arms. "I didn't believe I'd ever hear you say that to me."

"Why did you think I went to see you in Chicago?"

"I wasn't sure. I thought perhaps you were testing yourself. I knew you were sure as hell testing me. You were so beautiful, standing there looking so solemn. It was all I could do to keep from grabbing you right then and there."

"Did I look like you had imagined?"

"I knew exactly how you looked." He took her hand and gently tugged her down the hallway. "Come here. I have something to show you." He flipped on the light in the master bedroom and led her toward the bed. Taking her shoulders he turned her around. She stared at the walls in disbelief. There were giant pictures of her on the wall facing the bed—on the boat, on the terrace, laughing, looking pensive, and one of both her and Damon. She had been watching him while he explained something, his hands gesturing, his face alight, and the expression on her face caused her to blush. Her face shone with love for him. She shook her head, bewildered.

"Did Justin take these?"

"Yep."

"When did you have them blown up?"

"When I knew for sure that I was going to be able to see again. Justin brought me back to the lake to recuperate after the eye surgery. I decided nothing would help my eyesight improve quicker than the knowledge that I had you to look at, for hours, if I wanted to." He pulled her to him. "Those pictures kept me going during some pretty dark days, love."

"Why didn't you call me? I would have come down."

"Because I didn't want to pressure you. As far as I was concerned, you had decided not to get involved. I knew your feelings for me and that I could coerce you, for a little while, into being with me. But that's not what I wanted from you."

She turned and wrapped her arms around his lean waist, holding him close. "No, you were right. Although there was a time when I thought I would be contacting you."

"When was that?"

"When I thought I was pregnant."

She felt him stiffen in her arms, then he held her even tighter.

"Were you?"

"No, but I was several weeks late. I decided later it was nerves that had caused the delay."

"We took no precautions, though, did we?"

She shook her head, but refused to raise it from his chest.

"I'll admit I knew we were taking a chance, Elise. In fact, I even found myself hoping you were, because then I would have had a reason to insist we stay together."

"Even if you hadn't regained your eyesight?"

"Yes, even then. Had you been pregnant, there would have been an even exchange and you wouldn't have been marrying me just to look after me."

"That would never have been the reason, Damon."

"I know. But I have a fair amount of pride myself, you know."

She raised her head, her eyes rounded innocently. "No! I would never have guessed."

He popped her on the rear, then paused, gently rubbing the area. "Hmm. I didn't mean to bruise anything."

She smiled. "You didn't."

"I had gone in to make me a drink since I was having trouble falling asleep. Would you care for one?"

She shook her head, her eyes dancing. "You once mentioned a great sleeping pill we might try. I understand it's better than a drink and doesn't leave you with a hangover."

He grinned. "That's very true, but there can be some permanent aftereffects to that, as well. Are you willing to risk it?"

"Are you?" she asked.

"You're damned right. There's nothing I'd like better than to raise a family with you, the sooner the better."

She raised herself on her tiptoes. "Let me see if I can remember how those sleeping pills work," she murmured, brushing her mouth against his.

Damon scooped her up in his arms and in a few strides reached the large bed. Lowering her gently, he followed her down, his mouth possessing hers.

"You forgot the light," she whispered.

"No, I didn't. I want to see you, my love. I want to feast my eyes on every inch of you. There was no way I was going to allow Justin

to photograph you the way I wanted to see
you. I've waited long enough.'' He slipped the
gown over her head and tossed it to the floor,
his clothing following soon afterward.

Never had Elise felt more worshiped than in
the following hours. Damon touched every
part of her body with his hands, his mouth and
his tongue—learning her, experiencing her and
reawakening all of her body's needs. He allowed her the same freedom with him, and she
gained additional pleasure knowing that he
watched her enjoy him, her hands and lips
delicately touching him, arousing him until
they were both at a fever pitch of need.

One moment she knelt over his body, loving
him—the next moment Elise found herself on
her back, her hands held lightly above her
head, Damon on his knees between her thighs.
''You're a witch, do you know that, woman?
You've got me totally bewitched, and I can't
hold back for another moment.''

He stretched out above her, their bodies
touching, and she shifted, trying to free her
hands. When he let them go she placed them
around his neck, pulling him closer. She lifted
her knees, giving him access to her, and he en-

tered her in one, strong surge of masculine power.

She had forgotten what it felt like to be totally with Damon. Not even her memories could recreate the marvelous sensations that occurred whenever he was deep within her.

Their slow lovemaking had created a frenzy of desire within them both, and once joined together their need to express their love intensified until they were both swept away. Time and space no longer had meaning for either of them. It was enough that they were together. And when the release finally came, they enjoyed it together, holding each other tightly as they drifted back to this planet, at this time and moment. They were one.

Thirteen

Justin Drake pulled up in front of Damon's place at the Lake of the Ozarks and gazed out at the lake. It had been a while since he'd been there. More than two years had passed since Damon's near-fatal accident, and he and Elise had been married for almost that length of time. Or at least it seemed that way.

He couldn't get over the change in Damon since Elise had come into his life. He was more relaxed, and very little ever excited him, except for a few months ago when Elise had gone into labor a few weeks early. Then Damon had come practically unglued. It was amusing to think about now, but at the time, there had been nothing funny about the circumstances. They had all been worried. Elise, with her nursing background, better understood the dangers to the baby, but she was the one who had ended up trying to calm Damon down.

Justin climbed out of his car and stretched. The early-summer sun felt good to him, and he was already anticipating a little sunbathing. The front door stood open and he decided to check inside before looking for the Trents down near the water. He walked through the doorway and stopped, a large grin on his face. Who would ever have believed it?

Damon sat in a large rocking chair in front of the sliding glass door leading to the terrace, a small infant sleeping soundly on his shoulder. Damon glanced up and saw Justin and placed his finger to his lips. Justin nodded his understanding.

Carefully standing up, Damon disappeared down the hallway, presumably to place the young Damon Eric Trent in bed. When he returned he stuck out his hand.

"You're a sight to see these days, Justin.
What's with this growth under your nose?"

Justin grinned. "I decided to change my
image, so I grew a mustache. How've ya been,
Damon?" He shook hands with the man who
was like a brother to him.

"Can't complain. Why don't we go down to
the dock where Elise is sunning. Mattie will
listen for Eric." He paused. "Would you like
to change clothes?"

Justin glanced down. "That sounds great.
Give me a few minutes and I'll be on down."

When he started down the pathway to the
dock a few minutes later, Justin grinned at the
picture of Damon and Elise. She was in a
skimpy bikini that revealed no signs she had
ever given birth to a child, and Damon was
smoothing tanning lotion over her golden
midriff with a sensual enjoyment that made
Justin feel like a peeping Tom.

"All right, you two. Enough of that. Remember, my old bachelor heart can't handle
too much titillation these days."

"Justin! I didn't know you were here. When
did you arrive?" Elise sat up and removed her
sunglasses.

"Just a few minutes ago."

"And you've grown a mustache. I love it."

Damon looked first at his wife, then at his friend. "That's enough. You can like his mustache, Elise. You don't have to love it."

Justin and Elise laughed at the scowl on Damon's face.

"Come on, Damon. It's too late to be jealous of me. I had my chance to beat you to her while you were laid up in the hospital and I blew it." He grinned at both of them. "It was obvious even then that Elise had no time for anyone but you."

Damon finished smoothing the lotion over Elise's middle and capped the bottle. "That's right. So why don't you go find your own girl and leave mine alone."

Justin stretched out in the sun and sighed. It had been a long time since he'd had a chance to relax. "Maybe I will, one of these days. But for now, you keep me too busy for anything but work."

"It's good for you."

For the next several hours the men discussed business. In the meantime Elise went inside, planned their evening meal, fed Eric

and enjoyed seeing Damon and Justin together. They were good for each other.

Damon still put in long hours, but Justin did
more and more of the traveling so that Damon was home with her each night.

She had been surprised when he came home
a few days ago and suggested they come to the
lake. He'd been so fussy about taking Eric
anywhere until he was older, but now, at three
months, Eric had proved to be a congenial
traveler.

Her life had certainly been different in the
past two years. She had given up her job and
her apartment, moved to Chicago and shared
Damon's spacious condominium high over
Lake Shore Drive and Lake Michigan. Her life
seemed full to overflowing while she helped
out on a part-time basis at one of the downtown clinics, in between entertaining Damon's business acquaintances. Since Eric's arrival, her schedule had undergone additional
changes, but she loved her life, every moment
of it.

She had seen Cynthia on several occasions,
and although she knew they could never be
close she recognized that Cynthia accepted her

in Damon's life. Cynthia had even sent Eric a baby gift, which drew no comment from Damon.

Elise offered to prepare dinner that night and Mattie took the opportunity to go visit with friends. After dinner was over, Damon, Elise and Justin sat out on the terrace, enjoying their coffee.

"I really appreciate having a few days to come visit," Justin commented. "It's so peaceful. It's as though none of the rest of the world really matters when I'm here."

Damon smiled. "I know the feeling. I was getting frustrated with the delays in the Buenos Aires deal and decided, what the hell, we'd come down here for a few days and relax."

"I know. I'm going to have to go down there myself, I'm afraid." Justin raised his brows. "Unless you'd like to go, instead."

"Thanks, but no thanks. I've had enough of traveling for one lifetime. You can have it."

Justin glanced over at Elise, sitting quietly by Damon's side. "Mattie really outdid herself tonight, didn't she?"

"Mattie went out this evening, Justin. I prepared dinner."

He groaned. "Wouldn't you know it? Looks like a dream, intelligent, and can cook as well. It just isn't fair that Damon should get all of that. Too bad you don't have a sister."

Elise smiled, thinking of her feisty, vivacious sister. What a pair those two would make. "Oh, but Justin," she said with a mischievous grin. "I do."

*   *   *   *   *